Switched

By Iris Báijīng

Copyright © 2020 Iris Báijīng

ISBN: 978-0-578-76702-4

LCCN: 2020918090

First edition December 2020.

Edited by Alexandra Ott, Olivia Funderburg and Sirah Jarocki

Cover art by Leah Kerbs

Layout by Rachel Johnson

Content Warning:
Implication of depression, discussion of abandonment, and sensitive orphanage scenes.

To adoptees, you are not alone.

To Lin and Bethany, my original "orphanage sisters."

Switched

By Iris Báijīng

Prologue

A piercing cry escapes the lips of a newborn baby. "It's a girl," the nurse whispers.

Two years later

"What happened? I thought Huī Yīn was supposed to go with them..." the volunteer with red butterflies on her shirt pauses.

" – They didn't ask for a child with problems. They wanted a healthy girl." The nanny fidgets with her glasses. *"Yīng Yuè was always crying. She wasn't going to make it if she stayed here. She needed them more."*

"But they could have taken care of Huī Yīn. Doesn't she deserve a home too?"

"She needs to be tested. Something isn't right with her."

I don't understand what they're talking about. Is something wrong with me? I'm lifted up, and a man in a white coat says, *"It's going to be okay."*

Lights are in my face; cold objects are pressed against my skin. I see people lean in close. They poke and prod. I don't cry. I don't care anymore.

Part One

Chapter 1

Yìng Yuè (Leila)

Twelve years later

Are you here? I text Jasmine. Looking around, I don't see her anywhere.

On my way. Be there in 5. Meet you at the pool, Jasmine replies.

Late as usual. Oh well, I shouldn't have expected anything different, knowing her for as long as I have. I can't believe it's been six years since we started swimming together on the local YMCA team.

I remember my first day of practice. My mom had to bribe me with a new cake decorating set to get me to the pool. When I arrived, Jasmine was doing the splits on the pink stretching mats in front of the bleachers. She was all business with her fancy Speedo goggles and a sparkly rainbow cap that tried to contain her curly black hair. The moment she saw me, she practically ran in my direction and asked if I wanted to swim with her in lane two. We've been friends since, and it is rare to see one of us without the other.

Jasmine had been waiting for this day all summer. She wouldn't stop talking about finally being on the high school team and have people other than our parents cheer for us.

But where is my longtime swimming buddy? Of course, she's running late. I guess that means I will have to walk there on my own. Picking up the pace, I jog toward the pool.

Even though the distance from the school courtyard to the pool is only about 50 yards—I swim that distance all the time—I am already starting to break out into a slight sweat. Little drops of perspiration bead up on my forehead as I race with my duffle bag full of swim gear.

The beating sun overhead feels unusually warm on this late September afternoon. I make it to the pool just as the coach is gathering everyone together.

"Welcome to the high school swim team! For those of you I haven't met yet, I'm Charlie Garrett. You can call me Coach Garrett, but most people just call me Coach. I'm excited to be working with you! Let's meet our team captains and then we'll do an ice breaker in the water."

"Hi everyone, I'm Olivia."

Olivia looks to be nearly six feet tall with broad swimmers' shoulders and long legs. She is thin, but muscular and could easily pass for a basketball player. I wouldn't be surprised if she played other sports.

"And I'm Lacey."

Lacey is much shorter standing up there next to Olivia, but I suppose she is probably average in height. Maybe 5'3 or 5'4, which is much closer to my own height. Wavy chestnut hair frames her face. Despite the distance, I can feel her bubbly energy and outward friendliness.

"We're looking forward to a great season and can't wait to know you better!" Lacey says.

"If you have any questions about being on the team, you can ask us or the other returners," Olivia adds. She already appears to be bored with this whole introduction.

"Thanks, Olivia and Lacey. Now I want everyone to find a

partner. Find someone you don't know. Let's break some ice!" Coach Garrett chuckles to himself.

Oh, here we go. A coach who's trying to be funny. I wonder how long this will last. Jasmine snuck in during the introductions. She waves to me from across the semi-circle of swimmers that had formed. She is already paired up with someone I don't know. Now it's my turn to find a partner. I'm not sure how to approach the other girls, but Olivia spots me.

"Hey, you're Leila, right?"

I nod my head.

"I remember you from when I used to swim with the Y."

"Right...you and Lacey were both on it for a few years."

I had thought they looked familiar. It's coming back; Lacey and Olivia had been on the Y team when I had first joined, but they quit before they started high school. Since they were older than me, I didn't get to know them that well.

"Yeah. I remember you and Jasmine were very fast for your age," Olivia says thoughtfully. I think she is trying to remember just how fast we were and if we were a threat to her standing as captain.

"Thanks." My mouth turns up in a slight smile as I try to laugh off the compliment.

"Well, I'm glad you're both going to be on the team this year. We're all hoping we can make it to State."

It is hard to tell how sincere Olivia is, but she seems genuinely happy that maybe Jasmine and I could help her get to State.

"So, how hard is State?" I ask.

I had heard the times aren't too challenging if you are a club swimmer, and nothing compared to the National times Jasmine and I are aiming for.

"Probably not hard for you. It took me three years to break into the 25s for a 50 free. That's my main event, but it's the relay I'm trying to go in. If you're as fast as I remember, I bet we'll be on it together."

"I love relays!"

Something most people, with the exception of Jasmine, don't know about me is individual events still scare me. I try to keep it together, but I hate being in the spotlight. And when it's just me up there, I get shaky. My arms and legs start to tremor and my heart races like a hummingbird's.

It takes many deep breaths and some light stretching to stay calm. I have to block out everything and just focus on the lane in front of me. You would think that after six years of competitive swimming, I would have gotten over this anxiety by now. It never really went away, but I have learned to deal with it. While I can swim individual races, I much prefer relays if given the option.

"Introduce yourselves and then get ready for the wheelbarrow race. Remember, everyone needs to take a shower before entering the pool," announces Coach Garrett.

"How do we do a wheelbarrow race in the water?" I've heard of them on land, but in water?

"It's easy. Come on!"

Olivia hurries to the locker room to rinse off and I follow. After a quick shower, and trying not to slip on the wet deck, we jump into lane one. All the pairs are getting ready and spreading themselves out among the six lanes. I spot Jasmine, and she looks in the zone, ready for the friendly competition. Olivia gets into position with one hand on the wall.

"Float on your stomach with your feet toward me," she instructs.

I do what she says. She grabs my feet as Coach Garrett shouts, "Go!"

We are off. Powering us from behind, she uses her feet to propel us. I try to stay as streamlined as possible so we can glide through the water. When we are more than halfway across the pool, I can feel the momentum slowing down.

Olivia's kicking is feeling more labored and even though we are close, we need a little boost. We swiftly switch roles and I begin to kick. My legs get into the rhythm and I easily push us to the other end.

"Great job, ladies!" Coach Garrett claps his hands. "That was just your warm-up. Let's get started. I want new swimmers in lanes one and two, horses in lanes three and four, and everyone else in lanes five and six."

"Horses?" I look at her questioningly.

"That's the term Coach Garrett uses for the most experienced and fastest girls on the team. We're horses," Olivia replies.

We duck under the lane lines until we are in lane three with Jasmine and Kate, her new friend. Coach Garrett hands us the workout on a slip of laminated paper and we all huddle together to read it.

500 swim
200 pull
200 kick
3x200 free on 2:15
2x200 choice on 2:30
3x100 choice on 1:10
Cool-down

Okay, that doesn't look bad. For newbies, reading a workout like this might seem challenging, but it's actually quite simple. All the numbers in the hundreds just refer to distance. The pool is measured in yards, and one length is 25 yards. A 500 swim means 20 lengths of the pool and your choice of freestyle, backstroke, breaststroke, or butterfly.

Before we can figure out the swim order, Olivia takes off and leads the lane. Jasmine is right on her heels. Kate is third and then me.

Pretty soon, my arms feel like jelly, and my throat is dry. We stop at the end of the 200 pull for a quick water break and then continue with the 200 kick. I take a kickboard from the wall and my legs go to work. As I'm kicking, I glance around the pool. It's surprising how many girls are on the team. I would estimate there are at least five girls in each lane, with a good mix of brand new and more experienced swimmers.

We've only been swimming for about ten minutes and already my body feels warmed up. It's time to move on to the sprints.

Jasmine asks, "Who's leading?"

"I can." Olivia makes her way to the front and gets into position.

She leaves as the second-hand on the large poolside clock hits the 12. Around the third 200, Olivia is starting to lag. Jasmine catches up to her and Kate is right behind Jasmine. I'm still trying to keep my distance, so we aren't all swimming on top of each other.

I think Olivia is beginning to realize she might not be the fastest swimmer anymore. She lets Jasmine pass her, and Kate follows. I don't want Olivia to be annoyed, so I stay behind and give her some extra space. Soon, I can feel her wake when I pull my arms through the water. At the end of the second set of 200s, Olivia motions for me to pass her.

Just as we're about to complete our workout, my left leg gets a sharp pain in it. Ugh, it's a muscle cramp, and I need to stretch it out. But Coach Garrett calls us to the deck and I wearily pull myself out of the water. My arms and legs haven't felt this worn out in a long time. I'll admit, it was a good workout. Jasmine and I took a short break from swimming during the last few weeks of summer. We need to start getting back into racing shape.

"What a great practice! I'm excited to see where this season takes us. I think we have a lot of potential, and I know State is in the back of many of your minds. Let's keep up the good work, and I'll see you all tomorrow! Remember, there's an optional morning swim for those of you who want to push yourselves. Captains, anything you want to say?"

"Let's make this a year to remember! And have a wonderful first day of classes tomorrow. If you see us around campus, wave!" Lacey says.

Olivia chimes in, "Before you go, we're going to end with a quick cheer. Returners let's show our freshmen how it's done. Freshmen, repeat after us."

"Icky-la-picky-wicky"

"Icky-la-picky-wicky"

"Icky-la-boom-ba"

"Icky-la-boom-ba"

"Oh-waffle-doffle-doffle"

"Oh-waffle-doffle-doffle"

"Icky-la-boom-ba"

"Icky-la-boom-ba"

"Goooo Eagles!" we shout in unison.

Most of the girls rush to the locker room after the cheer. Jasmine, Kate and I stay to stretch a little longer on the deck. We can hear their noisy chatter and excited voices.

"Hey Kate, we're going to grab dinner at the food carts. Want to come?" Jasmine asks.

"Sure!" Kate pulls her arm over her head to stretch out her shoulder.

When we feel loosened up enough, and my leg, thankfully, feels better, we pack up our swim bags. As I open the locker room door, a huge wave of steam engulfs my face. We can barely get around all the girls in line for the showers. Luckily, there are still spots open in the back and we set our stuff down on the benches.

While waiting for the showers, I ask Kate, "How long have

you been swimming?"

"A little bit here and there."

"I haven't seen you around before..."

"—Yeah, I just moved here with my family."

"She's lived all over the US." Jasmine reaches for her shampoo.

"Really? Where?" I grab a towel from my bag.

"Oh, New York, Louisiana...Maine, and now Oregon."

Kate doesn't elaborate and I'm shy about asking. Maybe Jasmine has already asked her and she doesn't want to talk about it anymore. It is our turn for the showers, and we quickly wash our hair and change so we can go downtown and get some food. I am starving after that workout and feel like I could eat a whole casserole dish of my mom's famous eggplant parmesan.

Can you pick us up? I text my mom.

Moments later, she "likes" my message and sends the thumbs up emoji.

"So where are the food carts?" Kate asks.

"By Third Avenue downtown. Hopefully there's something you like," I say.

"Yeah, I'm not picky."

"Have you been downtown yet?"

"Not that much."

"We can give you a little tour." A silver electric Leaf pulls up. "There's my mom!"

"Hi, girls! You must be Kate." She smiles.

Kate nods and sits beside Jasmine in the back. I adjust my front seat to give them some more leg room.

Soon, I see the familiar rows of food carts lined up along the street. There are already crowds of people waiting beside the carts. The smoky scent of Mediterranean kabobs and stir-fried Pad Thai waft in through the rolled-down windows.

"Mm, that smells so good!" Kate says.

Jasmine inhales deeply. "Just wait until you try it."

"Thanks, bye!" I wave to my mom and close the door. We rush over to where the rows of tantalizing food carts are calling our names.

Chapter 2

Huī Yīn

Thirteen years ago

Age two

Talking

What is that sound?

My voice works

I don't want to stop

Why did it take so long to start?

I want to talk to everyone

Hi pretend friends

Let's play a game

Lights out

Time for bed

Goodnight babies

Nine years ago, age six

Survival

I did it!

They thought I

Couldn't survive

I believed in

Me

I overcame

Fevers and chills

Silence and solitude

Hunger and thirst

Abandonment.

I survived the impossible

I am alive

It's a new day

People come, people go

Surprise

Full of energy

Stay happy, or be sad

I am strong

Day After Day

Same thing

Day in, day out

Morning, night

Sleep, eat, repeat

Help with the little ones

Feed them, bathe them

Watch them, rock them

Clean, wash, dry

No Family

Visitors are coming!

Must be clean

Adopt me?

No

No one wants a six-year-old

I'm too old

No more

Smiles

Tears

Fall

Quiet

Calm

Alone

Chapter 3

Yìng Yuè (Leila)

We walk around to check out which carts are open and look good tonight. I'm immediately torn between the Middle Eastern and Indian food. My mouth is watering. Should I choose the char-grilled kabobs or the creamy chicken tikka masala?

"What are you thinking?" Kate looks over at us.

"I'm getting the chicken tikka masala," I say, satisfied with my decision.

"I think I want something vegetarian. How are the falafels?" she asks.

Jasmine looks briefly at the falafel cart. "Oh, they're good! Are you a vegetarian?"

"I'll eat some meat, but I try not to eat a lot."

"Got it. We could all get something and share?" Jasmine suggests.

We agree and plan to meet up at Challah for Ice Cream with all our food. While Jasmine and Kate are still in line to order, I stare longingly at the ice cream cart. Ice cream sounds good.

I watch as little kids carefully lick their giant scoops of chocolate and strawberry ice cream piled high on waffle cones. Waiting near the ice cream cart, I can't not notice the Challah Special. I deserve something sweet after the hard practice, right?

Kate and Jasmine come back with their hands carefully balancing loaded plates of veggie kabobs, falafels, dipping sauces, slices of grilled naan, and cups of frozen lemonade. The good thing about being swimmers is that we burn through calories. As long as we don't indulge too often, we're fine.

We walk toward the waterfront park because there's no open seating by the carts. As we are walking, Jasmine and I take turns pointing out some of our favorite hangouts.

A little pink trolley crosses our path. "That's the trolley that we used to love. We could go with you if you want. You'd be surprised how many 'older' kids still ride them," I say.

"There's the waterfront trail and the Willamette River." Jasmine points to where people are strolling along the scenic path. The evening sun is glistening on the water and small sailboats bob in the distance.

"We like to come down here and just relax." I take a quick bite of ice cream and mumble with challah in my mouth, "If you take the trail to Burnside, you'll end up at the Saturday Market. We should go sometime."

We find a place to sit down on the grass. With our piles of plates, it is hard to know where to begin. Jasmine has already started eating her kabob and Kate dips a falafel in her tzatziki sauce.

We are eating and laughing at YouTube videos Jasmine pulls up on her phone. In the background, the dramatic sunset reflects on the evening clouds. Tonight, it looks like one of my mom's oil paintings. It has streaks of amber and scarlet with flecks of pale pink poking through.

"So, is anyone nervous about tomorrow?" I hate first days; they are so unpredictable.

"Nah, not really." Jasmine is now scrolling through her Instagram stories.

"I've moved around so much; new schools aren't scary anymore," Kate says softly.

"Oh," I pause and then finally get the courage to ask, "Why have you moved around so much?"

"I told Jasmine earlier... I bounced around between relatives before David and Richard adopted me last year. We used to live in New Orleans, close to my uncle, but then David got a new job and so we moved here a week ago. I'm still getting used to everything."

"I was adopted too." I want to say more, but I don't know what.

Jasmine looks up from her phone. "There's your mom!"

We walk over to the car and, as I open the door, Charlotte pops her head out.

"Hi, I'm Charlotte!" She looks at Kate's gingery-auburn hair. "I love your hair! I've always wanted to dye my hair that color." Kate's hair reminds me of Anne's from *Anne of Green Gables*, but in a good way.

I nudge Charlotte to slide over.

"Oh, thanks. Yeah, it's kind of an unusual color." Kate fiddles with the ends of her hair.

My mom backs out of the lot.

"Where do you live?" I ask Kate.

She has to think momentarily and then responds, "1805 Taylor Street."

"Oh, we're practically neighbors. We can drop Jasmine off and then you."

We're quiet on the drive back. I think the busy afternoon and all the excitement is taking its toll. From the bottom of the hill, Jasmine's house comes into view. It is a raven black, three-story, Victorian-style house that's been in her family for generations. Every Halloween, her mom goes all out with the Target décor to create the perfect haunted house.

It's such a big place that Jasmine lives there with her mom and her grandparents. Her dad's been out of the picture since before I met her.

Kate's house is everything Jasmine's is not. It is a quaint little navy blue and white cottage with a modest vegetable patch. It looks like her family is trying to start a flower garden, but it isn't the right season for it. The calm cottage seems out of place among the rest of the vibrantly painted and mismatched houses that give the neighborhood its "Artist Grove" nickname.

Back at home, I unload my bag and hang my swimsuit and towel to dry. I climb the winding staircase to the room I share with Charlotte.

"Charlotte!" I say in exasperation.

"What?"

"Can you please keep your clothes on your side of the room?" I point to all her clothes scattered throughout our room.

"Oh, sorry. I couldn't decide what to wear tomorrow and needed more space to try on outfits."

"Okay, but I want to go to bed, and your stuff is everywhere." I sigh in frustration.

"Okay, okay, I'll put it away." She scrambles to pick up her scarves, discarded shirts, and the array of shorts that are littered on the floor and spread across my bed.

I brush my teeth and wash my face. Then I scurry across the cold wood floor and jump into bed.

"Hey Charlotte?"

"Yeah?"

"Have a good first day."

"You too."

It's so weird to think that it has already been two years since I was in Charlotte's place, about to start middle school. It's the beginning of something new for both of us. I can feel it.

As I'm closing my eyes, I get a strange chilling sensation down my arms. The tiny hairs feel like they're about to lift right off my skin. It's like they know something big is about to happen. Something that will change my life.

Chapter 4

Huī Yīn

Seven years ago

Age eight

Moving Day

We need
More space, a
Bigger building
Better supplies
Carry these
Move those
Take this
Don't drop it
Goodbye old home
I will miss
My familiar room
My old bed
The tiny bathroom
We all shared
The long tables
Where we ate
Meals together
My home
Salty water
Drips
Down
My
Cheek

Tweet, Tweet
Chirp, chirp, the
Birds are talking
Time to wake
The sun is up
First day
In
My new home
Get ready
I won't move
My bed is warm
But
I have to
Time to work
It's time to start the day
Okay.

Stray Cat

An alley cat sits

By

My window

Soft meowing

The cat is

Skinny

What do you eat?

I see myself

Where do you sleep?

Do you have a

Home?

A family?

Little cat, you

Fend for yourself

You and me

We could be

Sisters in

Another life

Stay with me

Tonight

School

I wish for
School
Like other girls.
I am stuck
Here
Caring for babies
What would I give?
What do I have?
I dream of
Learning
I want to read
I want to be heard
Can I be a
Doctor?
Artist?
I can do it,
I can.
No chance.
What if I hurt myself?
How will I get there?
I am a
Nuisance
I am trouble, an
Unwanted burden.
Sigh
Maybe next year
Maybe not

Chapter 5

Yìng Yuè (Leila)

"Leila, turn off your alarm!" Charlotte groans and rolls over, trying to go back to sleep.

I guess I should get up now, but the sun hasn't even come up yet. It's only 5:45, and I have swim practice at 6:30. School starts at 8:00. Some days I wish I had my sister's schedule so I could sleep in. Swimming isn't her whole life. She doesn't have to go to morning practice. Lucky her.

I jump around on the freezing floor because it's such a shock compared to the warm bed I left moments ago. I need to buy new slippers so my feet aren't always so cold.

Looking for my clothes in the dark while trying not to disturb Charlotte is tricky. Reaching for my phone, I turn on the flashlight to find socks that I forgot to set aside last night. I quietly close the door of our room and hurry downstairs.

As I'm about to leave the house, I take a breakfast cookie and banana from the counter. I can never eat anything this early. The snacks are for later. I'm glad that my swim bag and backpack are already packed because now I can just grab my stuff and head out.

My mom drops me off, and I run, sorry, I mean walk, to the locker room. There, I hastily change into my swimsuit, rinse off and step onto the pool deck where Coach Garrett is waiting.

I'm handed the varsity workout. Looks like our warm-up

is another 500 swim, 200 kick, and 200 pull. Morning swim is optional, and there are only about eight dedicated swimmers present. Olivia is swimming with Lacey in lane four, so I go to lane three which is still empty. Jasmine is leaning over her bag taking out her cap and goggles. She's actually on time for once.

"No Kate?" I shove my hair under my cap.

"Maybe she forgot?"

My mind is not ready for the cold water, but I brace myself and hop in.

Jasmine and I have always been pretty evenly matched. We're good at motivating each other to get through tough workouts. Today, as I'm pushing off the wall, I feel oddly awake. My body feels light, yet strong, and I'm ready for a grueling swim. Surprisingly, I'm not overly sore from yesterday.

One of the things I love about swimming is just zoning out and letting my mind wander. I try to breathe every third or fourth stroke and remember to get a strong catch at the end of my pull. This morning, I get in the groove and lose track of how much I've done.

I'm about to leave for another 50 when Jasmine taps my foot letting me know that we reached our 500 yards. It's time for the 200 kick. It's a butterfly day for me, but Jasmine's not having it. She despises fly and chooses to work on her backstroke. By the time I'm done with the warm-up, I feel ready for the real workout. It's a pyramid of sprinting and endurance training. Not my favorite, but not the worst either.

Coach Garrett and the assistant coach are working with the newer swimmers. Like yesterday, we're in charge of our own workout. We watch the clock in front of our lane and get ready to leave when the secondhand hits the 12.

"Three, two, one, go!" We swim side by side, splitting the lane and racing each other. I beat her to the wall after the first 50, but she catches up on the 100. We are a close tie for the 200 and she out-touches me on the 250. Jasmine enjoys swimming distance, while I live for the sprints. Even so, we're both working on being better sprint and distance swimmers.

We make it to the end of the main set and begin the cool-down.

~

As we get ready for the school day in the locker room, I turn to Jasmine, "So what do you think of Kate?"

"She's interesting. I like her."

"I hope we can all go to State."

"That would be fun."

"Hey, are you teaching lessons today?" I brush my hair back into a low ponytail.

"Yeah, I talked to Sarah about changing my schedule since our weekly meets are starting soon."

"Right, I need to do that too! How are you not nervous?" I ask Jasmine.

"I mean, it can't be that different from middle school. Same cliques, same people, just older."

I envy Jasmine's easy-going attitude. My nerves are getting to me. I can feel the rush of blood to my cheeks, and my heartbeat quickens just at the thought of entering through those heavy school doors.

We walk to the high school auditorium where students are lined up by last name to get their class schedules. It's supposed to be for people who missed orientation or need another copy of their schedule. I still have mine, so I wait with Jasmine. We stand in the line for Bs, Bs for Blechel.

I message Kate to see if she's here yet.

Over at M's, she texts.

Meet at the courtyard after schedules, I send in our group chat.

We arrive at the courtyard just as the morning bell rings. There are so many students standing around and blocking the path that it's hard to head to class. Kate and I have first period together, but Jasmine doesn't, so she tries to slide into the line of students going the opposite direction.

"See you at lunch!" she shouts as she disappears into the

crowd.

Sadly, this semester, Jasmine and I have no classes together. We're taking all of the same subjects, but we have different teachers. This is the first time we haven't had at least one class together. I wish I had her confidence as I prepare myself to walk into geometry with Mr. Myers. Luckily, Kate and I can help each other get through it.

Geometry is in the basement of Hamblin Hall. It's been renovated recently, so it's pleasantly welcoming. There are giant glass windows that let in natural light and the walls are painted a subtle shade of mint green.

Instead of the desks with the tiny tables that are never big enough, there are long tables with six chairs around each one. Students gradually trickle in and I immediately look for an open seat near the back. I hope I don't have to talk today. What I wouldn't give to be able to just fade into the background like a chameleon.

We make our way to the open seats under a window and sit down. There are some other girls I remember from middle school. Mr. Myers clears his throat and waits for absolute silence, which never comes, so he just starts talking and doesn't stop until a student raises his hand to go to the bathroom.

Mr. Myers explains the syllabus and everything we're expected to learn throughout this semester and into the second semester. I'm listening, but by page four of the handout, my interest dwindles. With my geometry textbook in front of me, I flip through the pages. The review chapter doesn't look awful.

After a long twenty minutes, Mr. Myers wraps up his attendance and bathroom policy lecture.

I hear, "Turn to page eight, and start with problems one through ten. You can choose to do all the odd or even numbers."

He's watching us closely as we open our books to page eight. It's only day one and already I feel like we're being scrutinized for how well we follow directions.

"Can we work with a partner?" someone asks.

"I want you to try on your own first. *If* you finish early, you can check your work with a partner."

Before I know it, the bell rings, and students are frantically packing up all their belongings so they can leave.

"Don't forget your homework when you come to class on Thursday," Mr. Myers reminds us.

What's my next class? Oh yeah, world history. I think it is on the east side of campus in the New Main building. That's right, it's on the top floor and with the five-minute break, I'll need to hurry if I want to use the bathroom and not be late.

Foot traffic is slow since we're all trying to navigate to our next class. I'm a little out of breath as I climb the stairs to the third floor. Even with all my workouts, racing across campus and climbing stairs isn't exactly easy. Hey, don't judge: running on land is a completely different story.

Mrs. Demore is greeting students as they come into her classroom, gentle jazz music playing in the background. I duck in under the crepe paper banners, and then my eyes search for a seat near the back. This time, I'm out of luck. All the back seats are taken and I'm left sitting in the second middle row. At least it's off to the side.

On top of each desk is a paper syllabus very similar to the one from Mr. Myers' class. The words, "Family History Project," catch my eye. It looks like a project that we'll be working on all semester. Being adopted, I've never thought about my adoptive family's history. I wonder what I'll have to do for this assignment.

Mrs. Demore's syllabus talk is nothing like Mr. Myers'. She turned it into a Kahoot! game and we have to read the syllabus in order to answer the questions on our devices. After the game, Mrs. Demore asks everyone to stand up and give a brief introduction. We are supposed to say our name, something unique about ourselves, and something we hope to get out of this class.

My palms are getting sweaty. I attempt to regain my breath control: in through the nose out through the mouth. When it's my turn, I can't look at anyone. I stare at the corner of my desk and quietly mutter, "My name is Leila, I was adopted, and I hope to learn about Chinese and US history." I sit down and hope people aren't still staring at me.

"Thank you, Leila," Mrs. Demore says.

Mia—I think that's her name—introduces herself. I patiently listen to the rest of the group, glad to have the attention off of me. The familiar bell sounds, and I slowly approach Mrs. Demore's desk.

"Leila, right?"

I nod.

"Is everything okay?"

"Um... well, I was wondering if I have to do the family history project... I don't know anything about my birth family and I'm not interested in learning about my adoptive family's history."

"Oh, are you sure you don't want to research your adoptive family's history? It could be interesting."

"Is there something else I could do?" I start picking at my nails.

"Well, do you know very much about your adoption?"

"No, not really." I shake my head.

"Would you like to do a project about your adoption? You could tailor this to be more centered around your story. How does that sound?"

"I think I would like that better."

"Great! Now I don't want you to be late." She looks at the clock above the door.

"Thanks, Mrs. Demore."

I make it through the rest of the day, with the only break being a too short a lunch with Kate and Jasmine. They seem happy enough with their classes.

As the final bell of the day rings, I am eager to go to practice. I practically run to the locker room, which is saying something since I am not a fan of running. There, I change into my other swimsuit and am the first one on the deck. Coach Garrett walks over to talk to me.

"Leila, I've been following your club swimming in the paper for a while. I was thinking... Even though you're just a freshman, I would like you to take on more of a leadership role within the team. You're one of our most experienced swimmers and your dedication is inspirational. Many of your peers and our seniors will be looking up to you."

Wait, hold on. Is he serious? Has he seen how I am around other people? I'm extremely shy, and Jasmine calls me introverted. I tend to focus on myself when it comes to swimming. I'm not exactly into all the team spirit stuff.

"Thanks Coach, but I don't know if I'm a leader. Wouldn't Jasmine be more suited for that? She's much louder and way more outgoing."

"You know, a leader doesn't always have to be the loudest person in the room, or in the pool, for that matter. Sometimes the greatest leaders are the best listeners."

What a cheesy thing to say. But I guess it could be true. It makes sense that leadership goes both ways.

"Thanks, I'll think about it."

I see Kate and Jasmine and we gather around lane three. We're waiting to see if Olivia will be joining us before we start our warm-up. She decides to continue swimming with Lacey and the other girls in lane four instead. It's not a big deal, but I wonder if she's upset that we all passed her last time. Oh, well. I guess we'll get the lane to ourselves.

Kate leads us through a smooth warm-up. She has an easy speed about her, and I try to keep up. Soon, I realize that Jasmine is trailing. I slow down so she doesn't feel like she's getting left behind. Jasmine notices that I am slowing down for her sake.

"Don't worry about me. You can pace with Kate." She waves for me to go ahead.

~

By the end of practice, my body is drained. I don't want to start teaching, but teaching means money. All of the high school girls leave except for Jasmine and me. This is our first year teaching swim lessons, and it's strange, but I'm not nervous. I did some pre-teaching training during the summer and now I feel almost confident in myself as a swim instructor.

My shyness doesn't carry over to teaching swimming. For some reason, whenever I get ready to teach kids, I feel at ease. Maybe it's because swimming is so second nature for me. Maybe it's because there's a part of me that wants to help them swim as fast as me one day. Whatever it is, my shyness seems to dissipate when it comes to working with children.

However, the end of lessons can't come soon enough. My little students are exhausting today. I have to keep reminding them not to go to the deep end without me. One boy tests my patience and I give him a "time-out" until he can listen to the rules. Other kids keep trying to jump on each other during the free time. I think I must have repeated the safety rules close to ten times in one lesson!

I am so ready to go home after two hours of teaching, but our old club coach convinces us to stay for half of practice. It is nearly nine when I walk through the front door.

"How was your day?" my mom asks.

I groan. Now, I have to give her a recap of everything that happened.

I leave out the more routine parts of my day but mention the most interesting thing from school. "In world history, I was going to have to do a family history project. But because I was adopted, Mrs. Demore said I could write about that instead."

"Oh, what part of your adoption are you going to write about?"

"I don't know all the details yet. Probably about before I was adopted and maybe after. I want to learn more about my life at the orphanage."

"Well, we don't know that much. The orphanage didn't know anything about you before you were left there. Maybe we can talk to your teacher to figure out what she's looking for."

"Yeah, okay. I'm so tired, I can't think about it right now." I climb the stairs to my room and almost forget to hang up my suits and towels.

"Charlotte, have you seen my blue dress?" I'm looking through my closet and don't see it anywhere.

"I didn't touch it."

"Are you sure? I can't find it."

"I haven't seen it since the BBQ last week."

"Ok...well if you see it, let me know."

I don't have energy to argue with Charlotte. I choose a different dress to wear to school tomorrow. It's a loose summer dress that I think will pair nicely with my fall boots. Right now, all I can think about is how good it will be to go to sleep. As soon as my head touches the pillow, I'm out.

Chapter 6

Huī Yīn

Six years ago

Age nine

Cleaning
Scrub, scrub
Wash, wash
Clean, clean
Rags, rinse, repeat
Floors, doors, rooms
Rags, rinse, repeat
Clean, clean
Wash, wash
Scrub, scrub

Babies
They are
Tiny
Helpless
They don't
Know
They don't
Understand
They
Cry
Sleep
Eat
Poop
Stink
Quiet
Loud
Still
Watch
Wait
I was one of them

Tears

There's no place for sadness
Tears are
Pointless
Unnecessary
I have no more tears
They are
Gone
I must move on
My heart hardens
A sliver of hope
Remains
I am a shadow of
Myself
Will I ever be adopted?
Will my life ever
Change?
Questions I think about
Things I try to hide
Tears

Rain

In my city,

Some days

It pours

Other days

It sprinkles

It can stop

As soon as it starts

I like the rain

It is calming

I hear it on the

Roof

I hear it against the

Windows

I wish I could

Dance

But my legs

Hold me back

What is wrong with me?

The rain fuels

Life

Why not me?

Chapter 7

Yìng Yuè (Leila)

It is just Kate and me in lane three this morning. It feels strange not having Jasmine there. She never misses practice. I'm so used to always swimming with her that today my mojo seems off. As Kate and I are about to leave, she sits back down and stares at the locker room door with a distant look on her face.

"Hey, is everything okay?"

"I was just thinking...You know, I lived with so many relatives before ending up here and..."

"—Oh, do you not like it here?"

"No, it's been nice getting to know you and Jasmine. And David and Richard are great. They do love me. But I miss being with my aunt. We still Facetime, but it's not the same."

"Yeah, I get that. What was it like living with your aunt?"

"We would go on so many adventures around the city together. She had a tiny apartment in New York City, but it felt like home. She and my mom used to be close until..." She pauses and gets a little teary-eyed.

"It's okay if you don't want to talk about it."

"No, it's fine... She got ridiculously busy with work and thought I should live with my grandparents. I had to move to Cumberland Center, Maine. It was fine, but they're a bit old fashioned. They're also kind of rich. I was put in a private boarding school, which I hated. You know, the girls there were such snobs. I never cared about all that fashion stuff, but even the youngest girls constantly bragged about the newest designer backpacks and riding outfits. Equestrian shows were a big deal."

"Wow, I've never been on a horse before."

"Being around the horses was my favorite part about Cumberland. But then my grandparents wanted to go travel the world, and taking me would have just been a burden." She sighs.

"I'm sorry." I sit down on the bench beside her.

"My uncle was next on the list of relatives. He was more like an older brother to me. He was a head chef at a little bistro, and he cooked the best fried chicken and biscuits. I thought I would stay with him until college..." Her voice takes on an accusatory tone. "...but his new fiancée didn't want to raise me with her two other kids. She thought three kids would be too much. And my uncle didn't think he could make enough to support all five of us. He promised to visit me...I haven't heard from him in a while."

I try to remain positive. "Maybe he can come to State?"

"Yeah. That would be fun." She takes a deep breath. "But lately, I've been thinking about my mom. I wonder where she is."

"Are you allowed to contact her?"

"She didn't leave any contact information, and my uncle was always worried it wouldn't be good for me."

Trying to change the subject, I ask, "So when did you start swimming? You're good."

Kate smiles. "I actually learned at that private boarding school, and I guess it just stuck. When I was with my uncle, we went to the beach a lot. This is my first year being on a real team."

"Wow, you're a natural!"

"Thanks. David and Richard have been supportive and try to come to all of our meets."

"Yeah, I've seen them sitting with my parents."

"Do you ever wish you could see your birth parents?"

"Uh, I haven't thought about it."

"When I was younger, I used to dream she would come back for me."

"I don't remember my birth parents," I say softly.

"Really?"

I don't want to get into this right now. The clock above the mirror reads 7:45. "Hey, we should probably get going."

"Yeah, sorry for all of this."

"It's fine."

We're quiet on the walk to the courtyard. I notice the maple trees are turning vibrant shades of red, orange, and yellow. Fallen leaves crackle under my feet. It's a crisp morning and the air is refreshing. It's a stark contrast from last year, when all you could see and smell was hazy smoke.

We approach our usual meeting spot. Jasmine is working on some homework. Her world history notes are spread out across the table.

"Hey Jasmine, we missed you at morning swim today." I sit down across from her.

"Yeah. I wasn't feeling well, and I had to finish that assignment for Mrs. Demore."

"Oh. Are you feeling better?" Kate asks.

"Yeah, kind of."

Ring!

"Ugh!" Jasmine shoves all her papers back in her backpack. "See you later." She walks away and puts her headphones in.

The rest of the day passes pretty uneventfully. But at lunch, Jasmine almost acts like she doesn't care about school anymore. Not that she ever loved school, but she always seemed happy enough while we were there. Maybe whatever bug she has is making her feel down.

After high school practice, Jasmine and I are collecting the kickboards and pool noodles for our lessons.

"Hey Jasmine, is everything okay?" I reach over to grab some extra goggles for my students.

"Yes, why?"

"You seem kind of off today."

"I'm fine. Let's get ready for lessons." She leaves to go set up her lane.

Is she really okay? I keep trying to think about what might be bothering her. Maybe she just needs to get some rest. Our schedules have been pretty intense lately.

I guess if Jasmine doesn't want to talk about it, I won't push her. Besides, my conversation with Kate got me thinking more about my birth parents and China. I don't know why, but it was never something I had wanted to talk about. But now that Kate is sharing so much about her family, I'm beginning to wonder about mine.

Chapter 8

Huī Yīn

Five years ago

Age ten

Sun, Part 1

It's hot today

I'm sweating

I do my chores

I clean

I cook

I feed the babies

I'm melting

I can't stand it

It's too hot

I need water

I want it to go away

Sun, Part 2

It's pretty today

A warm sunrise

I like it

I need it

I want to

Hold it

It fills me

How long will it last?

It makes me feel

Happy

Friends

Come join us!

Really? I can?

Yes, yes!

Okay, wait for me!

Hahaha you walk funny

Wait!

Let's go!

Please wait!

I'm coming

I want to join.

Books

Here you go
If You Give a Mouse a Cookie
I like cookies
I don't like mice
They scare me
Why a mouse and a
Cookie?
Cute pictures
I want a cookie
Thank you
It's mine
It's all
Mine.
If you give a mouse a cookie...
Look
That's funny!
I make up a
Story
Look at the words
I can't read them
I want to learn
I will try
Please
Teach me

Volunteers
They read to babies
I sneak in
I listen from the corner
I watch them
Do you want to listen?
I nod,
Yes, yes!
Once upon a time…
I pretend
I'm the hero
In my own story

First Lesson

I see you like books.

Do you want to learn?

I nod.

Let's start with A

A

A is for apple

This is an apple

Apple

A makes ahh

Ahh

Apple

Yes, that's it!

A is for apple

Two years ago, age thirteen

Puberty

My body changes

I gain weight

I am taller

What is happening?

I am always hungry

I sweat more

Do I smell bad?

I wish for a shower

Here, this will help

It's called de-odor-ant

I need bigger clothes

Goodbye

I have to go back to England
I'm sorry
I wish I could stay
Here, these are for you
Books!
You are doing really well!
The nannies say they will help you
Learn English.
I don't believe them
Goodbye.
She is gone

Chapter 9

Yìng Yuè (Leila)

A few weeks go by, and swim season is picking up. It's mid-October, and Jasmine's mom has already decorated their house for Halloween. She bought some gargoyle statues for an added creepy factor this year. Fake cobwebs and tombstones are spread out along their lawn. It's like a scene from *Beetlejuice.* If I were a little trick-or-treater, I wouldn't go near their house.

Yesterday, we took Kate to Haize's Pumpkin Patch and drank fresh pressed apple cider while looking for the perfect carving pumpkins. Afterwards, we watched Coraline, and attempted to carve Jack-O-Lanterns. Mine looked more like pumpkins that had been attacked by a rogue knife. When I got home, I left my pumpkins on our front porch. This morning I looked out the window and saw squirrel tails sticking out of them. I hope my pumpkins make it to Halloween.

Today, I am planning on working on that adoption history project. Mrs. Demore wants it to be a cumulative project in place of a final. Maybe Kate has some ideas on where I should get started. She's doing a project similar to mine because of her own adoption journey, but her story is very different from mine.

Hey, have you worked on the adoption project? I text Kate.
No, but I need to.
Want to meet at the library this afternoon and work on it?
Sure!
I meet up with Kate at the Multnomah County Library.

It is just fifteen minutes from our neighborhood, so it's fairly convenient. The library has a nice collaborative work space with lots of tables and big comfy chairs. I came here a couple of times last year to work on projects with Jasmine.

"Where should we start?" I open my backpack and take out my laptop.

"Mrs. Demore made it sound like the project was very open ended." Kate looks through her meticulously written notes. "We can pretty much research and write about what we want."

"I think I want to learn more about my life before and at the orphanage."

"Oh, that sounds great! I'm thinking maybe I'll write about what it was like living with all my different relatives before being adopted."

My phone buzzes. It's Jasmine.

Are you free? she texts.

Sorry, I'm working on the adoption project with Kate.

Oh, where are you?

We're at the library. You can come if you want.

Nah, it's okay.

Are you sure?

Yeah, see you Monday.

"Who was that?" Kate asks.

"Just Jasmine. I told her we were working on our projects."

"Does she want to come?"

"No, she didn't seem interested."

"Okay. Well, I'm going to draft some ideas. What about you?"

"I should have asked my parents if they could tell me anything about my time at the orphanage. I guess I can see if my mom's around."

I open my contacts and tap my mom's name.

"Hi, Leila."

"Hi, Mom. I'm working on my adoption history project. Can you tell me about what it was like in the orphanage?"

"Leila, I'm grocery shopping right now. When I come

home, we can look through the paperwork, but I don't think there's much information."

"Is there any way to contact the orphanage?"

"I'm not sure. You could google it. It was the White Cloud Orphanage. I can help you when I get home."

"Okay, thanks."

I google the White Cloud Orphanage, and the first thing that comes up is a website about heritage tours. I click on some more links and find an address and a phone number. It's an international number, so it'll be expensive if I try calling it.

I continue searching, but it's hard to find anything useful. Most of the sites that I find don't have contact information, just stuff about adopting and Chinese foster families. I check in with Kate and see if she's making any progress.

"How's it going?"

"Pretty good, I have a rough outline of what I want to write about. You?"

"Uh, not so good. I'm running into a lot of dead ends. I think I'm going to have to wait until my mom can help."

"Well, I think I'm done for now. Want to go?"

"Sure. We can take the bus back."

~

Charlotte and I watch cooking shows on the Food Network while we wait for Mom to finish shopping. We're watching our third episode of Iron Chef America when I hear the garage door opening.

After I help put away the groceries, I ask, "Can you show me where the paperwork is from the orphanage?"

"Here, come with me."

We walk downstairs to the office where she used to work. She opens a cabinet above the computer and pulls out a small stack of papers. She lays them on the office desk. I pick up the top document and see a picture of a toddler sitting at the head of a small round table.

"Is that me?"

"Yes, aren't you cute? We think you were sitting with some of the other girls from your sleeping room."

"I wonder why I'm sitting at the front like that."

"They thought you acted like a little leader." More about me being a leader? Was everyone talking about another girl? It just didn't seem like me.

In another photo, I'm wearing polka dot pajamas. "Oh," I laugh. "I'm kind of chubby here."

"I think it's just the pajamas that make you look that way. When we adopted you, you were very underweight for your age."

"So, how old was I when you and dad adopted me?"

"The pediatrician thought you were almost two based on your development."

"Did the orphanage know anything about me before I was left there?"

"No, all they told us was that they found you on the doorstep. There was no note, no letter. You were just wrapped in a warm knitted blanket."

"How old was I when I was left there?"

"They thought you were around a year old."

I skim through the papers and see another picture of me. This time I'm holding a tiny baby book. "Why does the name say Huī Yīn?"

"Oh, that's just what they called you."

"But I thought my name was Yìng Yuè."

"It was. It is... It's kind of complicated... Let's talk about it another time?"

"Okay..."

"I need to get dinner started. You can keep looking if you want. Just put everything away when you're done."

That's strange. Why didn't my mom want to talk about the name? I was simply asking why it said Huī Yīn, and she stopped talking. It was like she was uncomfortable about it.

Was she trying to hide something? Maybe I'm jumping to conclusions.

I open up an envelope with more pictures of what must be me as a toddler. One is of me standing in a crib with giant bars on the sides, in another I'm wearing a flowered dress and standing on a box, in the last one I'm holding a little plastic ring toy. Was I an unhappy baby? I'm not smiling in any of the pictures.

Then I pull out my old Chinese baby passport. It's a dark red booklet with the People's Republic of China emblem etched in gold on the front cover. It must be the passport I used to come to the US.

I open it. There I am, staring into the camera. I look so solemn. All of the regular information like name, sex, and nationality is listed under the picture... That's weird. The birthday says July 18th, 2003. But my birthday is December 28th, 2003. Why is my passport different? It doesn't make sense.

"Dinner's ready!" my mom calls from the kitchen.

I quickly put everything away and go upstairs. I don't say anything, because what would I say? I don't feel comfortable asking more questions when my mom didn't even want to talk about my name. But something weird is going on. Why do I have a different birthday on my baby passport? Why is the Chinese name different on the pictures?

That night, I sleep uneasily. I toss and turn, unable to find the right position. I am thinking about the mysterious name and birthday. I wake every hour and for once, I am grateful for my alarm.

Chapter 10

Huī Yīn

One year ago
Age fourteen

Visitors
Hello
Hello
Where are the babies?
There they are!
I sit in the
Shadows
I watch
I wait
No one wants me
I am too old

I Miss

I miss when I was

Younger

When people

Saw me

Visited me

People

Forget

People go

They don't care

The Secret

It's all a secret
No one tells me
Whispers
People
Nurses
Doctors
Talk
They point
They nod
They shake their heads
They frown
Doors close
Curtains
Close
What is happening?
Why can't I know?

Thinking

I remember when the
Director would visit
He said I was
Smart
If I weren't an
Orphan,
I would go far
I pretend
It was a
Mistake
My parents are
Searching
They
Want me
Find me
I go home
It's a dream
A
Wish
I am
Unadoptable.

Memories

I remember

Another

Girl

She was

Always crying

Younger

I saw her

I watched her

One day

I was

Chosen

Dressed   I was

Picked   Not

Then   Swaddled

Hugged

Left

Replaced

She

Took my place

It was supposed to be

Me

Why her?

Where is she?

Does she

know?

I will never

Know.

Birthday

Happy Birthday
I don't know
Why people say that.
I don't know my
Real day of
Birth
I don't know
Where I was
Born
The girls are excited
They want the gifts
Foreigners bring
What do I want?
I don't know.
Maybe a
Family.
A way to
Get around.
I wish for
School
Can I?
Please?
I promise to be
Good.
I will do extra cleaning.
No.
The day is
Over
Am I
Fifteen today?
Happy Birthday.

Chapter 11

Yìng Yuè (Leila)

Before our Saturday practice, I text Jasmine to see if she wants to go shopping with me for Charlotte's birthday gift. She's basically a second sister to Charlotte since we have known each other for so long. I get the "..." symbols indicating that she's typing something. Then the dots disappear. There's no response.

Jasmine doesn't show up for practice either, but as I'm leaving, I see her talking to one of the boys from the high school wrestling team. She seems to be in an argument with him. I'm not sure whether I should go over there and talk to them or walk away. After about a minute, the guy leaves, and I decide to talk to Jasmine.

"What was that about?"

"Nothing!" she snaps.

I don't believe her.

"Leila, would you please just mind your own business! I'm so tired of all your nagging. You're acting like my mother! Why don't you go hang out with your new bestie, since you seem to like her so much better than me."

Jasmine stomps off before I can get a word in. Her response doesn't make sense. She's never yelled at me like that before. We have gotten into small arguments in the past, but they were never this intense. This one seems different.

I was just trying to be her friend. She's been acting so weird lately, skipping practice, not responding to texts. Don't best friends look out for each other? We used to always confide in each other.

Am I being overly concerned? If I'm being honest, maybe I'm kind of jealous that she isn't spending as much time with me as she used to... *Before* high school. Maybe I have been spending more time with Kate, but that's because Jasmine's been off doing who knows what. I wish she would tell me what's going on.

I feel like there's so much drama in my life right now. When did I become the center of it all? Ugh. I leave the pool and take the bus to the mall. While I'm shopping for Charlotte, I run into Kate and we talk for a bit. I've only known her for about two months, but we've gotten close. Okay, I guess Jasmine does have a point there, but still...

"Hey, have you noticed anything off with Jasmine?"

"Not exactly... But she hasn't been as talkative as she was when I first met her."

"Yeah."

"She seems to be keeping more to herself."

"After club practice, she got mad at me for being concerned... I saw her talking to some guy from the wrestling team and it seemed like they were in an argument."

"Oh. I've seen her hanging around the wrestling team a lot lately. Maybe that's why she's been missing practices?"

"Maybe. Hopefully we can work it out."

Kate helps me pick out Charlotte's presents, and then I go home. I try to study for my geometry test, but I can't focus. Instead, I bake some chocolate cupcakes for Charlotte. It's one of my go-to recipes from the Food Network. I adapt it and add a little more cayenne pepper since she loves spicy hot chocolate.

As I'm taking the cupcakes out of the oven, the doorbell rings. I put the cupcakes on a cooling rack and run to get the door.

"Jasmine!"

"Here, this is for Charlotte." She practically shoves me a gift wrapped in walrus birthday paper.

"Hey, I feel like there's something going on between us." I'm playing with the ribbon on the gift.

Jasmine pauses. "Ever since Kate came, it seems like you just want to hang out with her. And in the pool, I feel like I can't keep up with the two of you. She's more your speed. I almost feel like swimming isn't my thing anymore."

"What are you talking about? You are my best friend. You're like a sister to me." I catch my breath. "And with the swim stuff, I thought you loved swimming. You're still one of the fastest on the team, and we need you for the relay."

"I know, but we've been swimming for so long. Don't you ever get tired of it? I want to try something new."

"Oh. But what about the rest of the season? What about State?"

"Yeah, I know."

"Is something else bothering you? I'm sorry if I seemed overly worried earlier." I look down at the gift in my hands.

"Yeah, that was Kyle. He's on the wrestling team, and I met him in Econ. We were partners for a project and kind of just clicked."

"What happened today?"

"You know, he's been wanting to hang out a lot more and go to all these cool events downtown. I told him that with my schedule right now, I can't. I barely have enough time to get all my homework done." She sighs.

"Is that part of why you don't like swimming as much? I know it takes up so much of our time, but just think of our goals. We used to dream about being college swimmers and going to Nationals. Don't you still want that?"

"Yes and no. I think those were more your dreams than mine. I want a more normal life. I want to be able to stay up late or pull an all-nighter. I want to go to parties with friends; I want to have my weekend free and not worry about waking up early for swim meets or extra practices. I'm so tired of swimming day and night with no time for myself."

"Oh... Are we okay?"

"Yes, we will be. I'm sorry I got mad at you today. I think I feel like I have no control over anything anymore. For so long, my mom has been pushing this swim thing. And seeing you and Kate get better while I'm stuck at my old times, I felt like I was losing you and swimming."

"Jasmine, I didn't realize that."

"It's okay. I feel better now that I'm talking to you about it. I just need some time to process everything. I'll see you on Monday. Say happy birthday to Charlotte for me."

"Okay, bye." I close the door and walk back to the kitchen to start decorating Charlotte's cupcakes. I pipe on some chocolate ganache flowers and get lost in my thoughts.

So there has been something going on with Jasmine. I knew something was wrong but didn't know how to help her. I feel like a terrible friend. I guess I've been so focused on swimming and my own worries that I hadn't realized how unhappy Jasmine was at the pool. I still hadn't gotten around to asking my mom about the passport birthday and the other name. Maybe it's not a big deal. What if I never say anything?

"I'm back!" announces Charlotte as she closes the door behind her.

"How was the mall?"

"Great! We went to the movies and got the extra-large popcorn and sodas. We even snuck in some of our own candy and didn't get caught," she says, satisfied with her slyness. "Then Melany and Skye bought me some new t-shirts and perfume. Look!" She dances around in a new shirt with the Avengers on it.

"Oh wow, that's really nice! They must have spent a lot on you. Make sure you thank them."

"I know Leila. You can stop being Mom."

"Sorry, I guess it's just a habit." Maybe I am becoming my mom.

"I can't wait for dinner at the HUB. Pesto chicken pizza

and cheesy breadsticks... Mm something smells good!"

"Oh, surprise!" I hand her one of the cupcakes. "I'll give you the rest of your presents tonight."

"Aww thanks!"

Charlotte's birthday dinner is a success, and she loves her gifts. That night, I think more about what Jasmine said. I realize it might be good for her to take a break from swimming, and I want to be there for her.

But *me*? I need swimming. It's been one of the only things helping me stay sane this past month. I'm just glad Jasmine and I are going to be okay. Now if only I can figure out what the story is behind my mixed-up Chinese passport. I'll talk to my mom about it, eventually.

Huī Yīn

Chapter 12

age fifteen

The Present

I feel my life isn't my own

I didn't deserve this

What if

I were adopted?

What if

I had a family who

Loved me

Cared for me when

I was sick

I wish, but no

I age out at

Fifteen

We're sorry, but we can no longer

Keep you here.

You have to

Move on.

Shock

I never knew that being fifteen means
I could never be adopted
I will never have
Happiness
A real home and
A family.
I pack my single bag
My one dress
I move out
I go to the
Senior center
Down the road
They knew
I would be coming
They give me a room
"Welcome"
I cry myself to
Sleep.

Name
Huī Yīn
That's my name
I always thought it would
Bring me glory
Or
Fame
That's what it
Means
But what I have is the
Opposite
I am
Poor
Nothing
No one

Senior Home

Welcome home

I am a nurse for the

Elderly

I live

Here

This is my

Life.

Music
What is that?
It's old
Small
Dusty
Can I touch it?
It makes
Sounds
That's deep
That's high
It has
Strings?
Keys
This is
Fun
What am
I doing?

Piano

I hear more sounds
What is it?
Someone is touching the
Music thing
Her hands move
Fast
I watch
I listen
Can I try?
Here
Play this key.
Yes, that's it
Now try this
Good, good!
Do you like it?
I nod
Can I keep
Playing?
Will this last?
This is called a piano
A pi-a-no
I can teach you
Thank you

Dreams
Hands fly
Black and white
Music everywhere
I am
Weightless

Chapter 13

Yìng Yuè (Leila)

Each day is getting shorter and darker. It's becoming increasingly harder to get up for morning swim. At the beginning of the month, Kate told me that November is National Adoption Awareness Month. I think she's doing something with David and Richard to celebrate her adoption day.

We've been texting a lot lately. It's nice having someone to talk to about being adopted. Jasmine's great, but with Kate, I can talk about adoptee things. It's oddly comforting knowing someone else has gone through something somewhat similar to me.

And no, I still haven't spoken to my mom about the birthday and name. Why? I don't know. Maybe I subconsciously think that the truth is something I don't want to hear. Maybe this is my mind's way of protecting me. Who knows.

I've been trying to focus on swimming. All the big end-of-season meets are coming up, and I want to do well. The District Championships for high school swimming are less than three weeks away.

It is after another draining Monday practice that Jasmine seems especially unhappy.

"I just can't do it anymore."

"I... know."

"I just don't love it anymore. Even the thought of going to the pool makes me feel kind of sick."

"Maybe it's time for a change?"

"Yeah, I tried to stick with it. I wanted to go with you and Kate to State. But I just don't get the same joy I used to."

"What do you want to do?"

"I think it's time to talk to my mom."

"Do you want me to go with you?"

"No, it's okay. I think this is something I need to do myself."

"I'll miss swimming with you, but I think you're making the right choice."

"Thanks. I'll let you know how it goes."

~

Mom's not happy. She thinks I'm throwing away everything I've worked for. But I'm just not happy. I won't do it anymore... Ugh... Jasmine texts. *She finally gave in, tell you more tomorrow.*

I'm sad Jasmine decided to quit swimming, but I saw it coming. Her heart isn't in it anymore. She isn't the same charismatic friend I have known for so long. At least, not when she's near water.

The following day, I can already see her personality returning.

"I'm trying out for the cheer team!" Jasmine says at lunch.

"What?" I ask, my mouth full of peanut butter and jelly.

"The cheer team has some openings and I want to try out for it. Will you come?" Jasmine looks at both of us.

"Sure, when are tryouts?" Kate asks.

"This Friday after school."

"We'll be there!" I say.

How strange; cheer was something I never knew Jasmine was into. Luckily, Friday is an early release day, so Kate and I will be able to support her.

~

After just a few days of practice, Jasmine looks like she isn't having any trouble keeping up with the tryout routine. Maybe she has some of her mom's gymnastics DNA flowing through her. Her jumps are right on the beat, and her landings are solid. She said something about wanting to learn how to be a "flyer" since she's on the smaller side. At least, I think that's the term she used.

After the tryouts, we meet up.

"Well, what'd you think?" Jasmine asks. She is still running on adrenaline.

"You were amazing! I can't believe you learned all of that in just a couple of days," I say.

"Thanks! I hope I make the team." She takes a drink from her water bottle.

"I don't know why you wouldn't. When do you find out?" Kate asks.

"This weekend, we'll get a call from the captains. And you know what? Robotics club isn't that bad."

"Wait, what? Robotics club?" I laugh.

"Yeah, I promised my mom I would try to stick with cheer and robotics the rest of the year."

"How did I not know you were interested in cheer and robotics?" I question her.

"I was kind of afraid to tell you. They aren't things you like, and I wasn't sure if I would like them."

"Oh. But you do?"

"Yeah, they're a nice change."

"Are you going to keep teaching?" I ask.

"Yeah, I want the money... I should probably check in with the team."

"Okay, I guess I'll see you at lessons."

Kate and I walk to the pool and Jasmine stays behind to talk to the cheer team. I'm happy she's found new passions. I'm going to miss my old swim buddy. But I have Kate, and together, we're making Lincoln history.

We're setting personal bests in all our events. We (well mostly Kate), have been breaking some of the ten and twenty-plus year-old school records. The local paper calls us the new

Water Duo of Lincoln High.

Kate is nominated for High School Swimmer of the Year. She's on her way to winning State if she keeps dropping time. In relays, we swim with Olivia and Lacey, who are the next fastest on the team now that Jasmine is gone. Hopefully at Districts we can qualify for State. Our relay is so close to qualifying.

~

I started developing a cough on the Monday before prelims roll around. What is it with bad news on Monday?

On Tuesday, I have a raging fever. Obviously I have to miss school. I'm hot, no cold...clammy, then sweaty. I lay around in bed all day and doze off here and there. I hope it's just a 24-hour flu.

I can hear my mom talking to my dad on the phone. She's worried because my fever still hasn't gone down all day.

"I think I should take you to see a doctor," she says.

"Do I have to?" I feel so weak I can hardly readjust my pillows.

My mom has to practically drag me to see a doctor at the urgent care clinic. I get a chest x-ray, and I'm diagnosed with pneumonia. The doctor gives me antibiotics and tells me to take the rest of the week off.

She doesn't want me spreading my pneumonia around the team and neither do I. But, it's not fair. This pneumonia has come at the worst possible time. Why did I have to get pneumonia? Who even gets pneumonia anymore?

That night, it is hard to sleep because I'm still coughing a lot. I can't take deep breaths without that gross yellow-green phlegm getting stuck in my chest. I've lost my appetite and can only stomach light fluids like chicken noodle soup and applesauce. On the plus side, I get to watch T.V. all day, but there's only so much Food Network and applesauce a person can take.

Saturday comes too soon. I'm still in recovery, and the doctor thinks it would be best if I stay home. From my room,

I am able to watch Districts because Portland Sports wants to highlight all the rising talent.

By "rising talent," I think they mean Kate. Not surprisingly, she makes it through prelims as the number one seed. Olivia and Lacey even make it to finals. It's well deserved, but the results are bittersweet. I so badly want to swim with my team.

The KGW does a pretty good job broadcasting the event. When it is time for our team to race, I cheer as loudly as I can. Given my pneumonia, my cheers are not very loud, but still, it's the thought that counts.

The suspense of the medley relay is nearly unbearable. It is just two minutes of swimming, but I can't take my eyes away from the screen. Kate leads off with a strong back time, coming close to her personal best. Lacey swims breast and Olivia fly. They have good times but don't come close to the times I have been swimming most of the season.

One of the juniors, Sirena, is swimming my place on the free leg of the medley relay. When she dives in, it doesn't seem like the team has a chance of placing in the top three. We are sitting in maybe fifth place. It is down to hundredths of a second; Sirena powers through to the wall... and our team comes in second!

During the award ceremony, Kate is standing at the top of the podium for all of her events. Again, the green-eyed monster makes it hard to stay positive, but I know she has earned her medals.

~

By the following Monday, I'm feeling much better and need to get back into racing shape for State. Just missing a week can make a big difference. After a long day of practice, I'm sitting on the edge of the pool trying to catch my breath. My lungs don't feel like their full capacity has returned yet.

"How are you doing?" Coach Garrett asks.

"Okay. I'm still not 100 percent."

"You're looking stronger, though. We're going to have a

time trial before we leave for State to see who will swim the 50 free in the medley."

"I don't know if I'm ready."

"Just do your best. We're all proud of how much you've improved this season."

"Oh, thanks." I laugh awkwardly. I don't do well with compliments.

~

Before falling asleep, I text Kate, *I don't think I can do it.*

Yes, you can. You just need to get your strength and endurance back.

I wish I had more time.

It'll be okay. Even if you go as the alternate, you still have your 50 free.

Yeah, but it's not the same.

Just try to stay positive.

Okay, talk to you tomorrow.

I have just two more days to rest and practice before the race to determine who will be in the relay. With State so close, I'm growing anxious. I guess it wouldn't be so bad if I go as an alternate, but it's not the same. I've worked so hard all season, and I want my chance to swim with the team. I have already qualified in the individual 50 free, but my favorite events are the relays.

~

I can hardly focus on my classes. People I don't know are wishing me good luck at State. Before getting on the bus, Sirena and I will race one last time. I'm feeling stronger. Maybe I can beat Sirena. We'll just have to wait and see. At the pool, the team gathers around. Sirena and I step behind our blocks.

"Good luck," I whisper before taking my mark.

Beep! The buzzer sounds.

We dive in.

Today is not my day. Maybe I'm still run down; maybe it is

my mindset. Sirena beats me by two tenths of a second. I reach over the lane line to shake her hand. It's something swimmers do after a race to congratulate each other. She is elated. I'm happy for her, really, but at the same time, I'm disappointed in myself.

Sirena and I throw on some clothes and get in the minivans the high school rented. We drive to the Tualatin Hills Aquatic Center in Beaverton where the State Championships will be held.

It is a short 30-minute ride, and when we arrive, my heartbeat quickens. There are rows upon rows of bleachers and three pools in this one facility, two racing pools and a warm-up/cool-down one.

The atmosphere is electrifying. Many of the teams have girls who are swimming some of the fastest times in the country. I'm sure college coaches will be watching us swim this weekend. No pressure.

That evening, all the teams are allowed to practice in a racing pool for one hour to get used to the new setting. The water is much colder, and the blocks feel higher and a bit wider than the ones we train on. We do some practice starts and finishes to end our session.

~

One perk of going to State is staying overnight at a hotel; a necessity since the meet starts early in the morning.

"So, what do you think of the pool?" I ask.

Kate yawns. "It feels fast."

"I think it's good." Olivia stretches her arms.

"We're going to do great!" Lacey says.

Sirena has fallen asleep.

I whisper quietly, "I'm nervous for tomorrow."

"Me too, but we can do it. We've been training so hard all season—" Kate begins.

"You've been swimming for what, six years? You'll be fine," Olivia says in the most supportive voice I have heard.

Coming from her, that means a lot. I think that in these past few days of intense practice and training we have started to bond more.

"Thanks. Good night." I turn off the lamp on the nightstand.

~

After our quick warm-up, Coach gathers us. "Alright girls. This is your time to shine."

As if on cue, the star-spangled banner starts signaling for the medley relay to get ready. Kate, Olivia, Lacey, and Sirena line up behind the blocks and say words of encouragement to each other.

In the same order as at Districts, Kate is the lead off, Lacey second and Olivia third. Sirena is about to dive off the block, and our team is trailing pretty far behind in sixth place. Her job as anchor is to push everything she has into her swimming and bring home our relay. Even with her best time, she still can't pull us ahead of the top four teams. As her fingers slam into the wall to stop the clock on the touchpad, she looks up to the scoreboard.

She has only managed to move us into fifth place for this heat. There is still one more heat to go, and with faster seed times, it's unlikely our team will make it to finals. The group looks crestfallen. I know they were hoping to place in the top three, but it was a long shot. Still, they hug each other and wish me luck.

The 50 free is up soon and I need to get mentally prepared. Kate will also be swimming the 50 free, but she is in the heat after me. As we wait for our heats to be called, Kate and I go through our pre-race ritual, jumping up and down and stretching our arms to get our bodies loose.

"We can do it!" we shout at the same time.

The warning whistle blows, meaning I need to get into position. I step onto the block with my head down. My hands and one foot are over the edge. I'm ready. *Beep!*

It is my quickest reaction yet; I dive in and my body knows

what to do. All that diving practice has paid off. I get into my rhythm immediately. Four quick butterfly kicks and then my arms start their pace of a 1:3 pull to kick turnover. I feel like I am building up speed as I near the wall for the turn.

I enter my turn with so much speed that I feel the momentum carry over when I push off the wall. I can't tell where the other swimmers are, but I know I must be going close to my personal best speed right now.

There are only 20 yards left. I take a quick breath and keep my head down as I power into my stroke. I reach with all of my might, focused on a full catch. My strong, light kick is helping me maintain rhythm through it all.

I don't breathe the rest of the way and slam my fingertips into the touchpad. I have never felt so fast. I take off my goggles and look up at the board to read my time.

I see a 24.90 by my name. I have never been below 25 seconds, and even Kate hasn't been that low. Kate is grinning from ear to ear and hugs me as soon as I get out of the water. I'm still in shock.

I watch Kate race and cheer for her, but she's edged out of the top six. She won't be swimming in the finals with me. Fortunately, she qualifies in her 100 back, so tomorrow will be another exciting day for both of us.

~

Kate and I wake up ready to swim our final races of the season. We go to the pool with Coach Garrett to warm-up. I feel strangely calm today. Have I gotten over my nerves? Who would have thought that would happen at one of the biggest meets thus far?

I hear my name being called, and it is my turn to walk out onto the deck. All six finalists line up behind their blocks.

"Take your mark."

Beep!

In a matter of milliseconds, my fingertips enter the icy water, my elbows next, then my face. Before I know it, I'm entirely submerged. My body knows what to do. Years of training have prepared me for this race.

The 25 flies by. Already, I'm at the wall getting ready to flip turn as fast as I can. I can feel it. My body is flying through the water. Just a few more strokes before I'll need to finish strong. I see the touchpad. No more breathing, my head is down. I am focused on my goal. I drive my fingers to the wall and look up at the board.

My time reads 24.50.

I shaved off four tenths of a second to place second! I can't believe it. Energy is still coursing through me. I don't feel tired at all.

It's now Kate's turn, and she is laser focused. Beep! Her backstroke is flawless. She glides through the water and leads the group. The girl in lane three is catching up to her. I hold my breath.

Kate manages to hold on. She wins the 100-yard back with a new personal best. She's practically jumping up and down when she climbs out of the pool.

Our whole team is cheering, "Goooo Eagles!"

When I look up into the stands, I see Jasmine waving. She made it and is sitting with my family.

At the end of all of the events, the medal ceremony begins. We wait to take our place on the podium. I proudly step onto the second-place level. My medal is placed around my neck and I thank the meet director.

There's one more round of congratulations, and Olivia, Lacey, and Sirena leave with their families. Now, it's just Kate and me.

Coach Garrett walks over. "I have some exciting news for you."

"What is it?" we ask.

"Let's wait for your families to come down here."

Our families meet us on the pool deck. I'm still feeling the excitement from today's results. I hardly comprehend what is said.

"You've been invited to swim and compete in China. It's part of the Oregon State Cultural Exchange Program, and you'll be swimming against the best provincial swimmers in Guangzhou!" Coach Garrett can hardly contain himself.

"Wait, what?" I ask.

"Really?" Kate looks like she is about to cry tears of joy.

My parents are standing there, quiet. It's hard to read their expressions. I'm not sure if I heard correctly. Did Coach Garrett say *Guangzhou*? That was where I was adopted. It was where I was probably born. I feel dizzy. I'm starting to get lightheaded.

"I know this is a lot of information to take in. The state coordinator wanted me to pass this on to both of you because of your great achievements this year. He'll be sending you and your parents more information soon," explains Coach Garrett.

I feel like I am in a dream. Is swimming going to help me go back to my birthplace? From the looks on my parents' faces, we have a lot to talk about. I think I sort of black out a little from all the news. I don't remember much after that.

Sleep doesn't come easily. Not because I'm not tired, but because so many things are swirling around in my head. I can't think straight. What would it be like to go back to the city where I was born?

Chapter 14

Huī Yīn

age fifteen

Piano Lesson
Good morning!
My name is Rose
What is your name?
Huī Yīn
That's pretty.
I want to teach you
This is C
Play C
C, C, C
Good, this is also C
C, C
It's higher.
Is this C?
C, C,
Now find all the Cs
Good, good!

Rose
She is
Kind
She lives here
She doesn't seem
Old
She loves music
It's part of her
Rose is my
Teacher

English

The volunteer at
White Cloud
Taught me
ABCs
Then she was
Gone
I miss her
I want to
Learn more
Reading
English is the way
Out   Me
English will help   I can do this
                          Study, teach, learn
                          Who will teach me?
                          How will I learn?
                          I practice writing
                          A, B, C, D, E, F, G
                          I can't remember
                          H or I?
                          Sigh
                          I wish
                          I could go to
                          School
                          I had a
                          Teacher

Practice

I love piano
I live for the
Music
I feel whole when
I play
Rose teaches
She says I'm
Improving
She pushes
I practice
And practice
I want to be
Like her
Her fingers are
Strong and
Powerful
I watch them play
I listen

English Classes

A sign
I read the Chinese
Community center
English classes
Are they
Free?
Can I go?
I want to learn!
I will go.

Hello

Hello,

Can I help you?

I want to learn

English?

Yes

Classes are at night

Okay

How much?

1,000 a month

That's a lot

I will never make

Enough

I start to leave

Wait!

How much do you have?

Not enough

What if we trade?

I will teach you

Can you teach me

Chinese?

Yes, yes!

Thank you!

I smile

I can do this

I will do this

Part Two

Chapter 15

Yìng Yuè (Leila)

Around seven a.m., the highly anticipated email arrives from the Oregon Cultural Exchange Coordinator. It reads:

> *November 23, 2018*
>
> *Dear Leila,*
>
> *Congratulations! The Oregon Cultural Exchange is excited to invite you to be part of the 18th Student Delegation to Guangzhou, China. The Oregon Cultural Exchange was organized in 2000 as an educational program to promote cultural awareness and appreciation through international travel and competition.*
>
> *During the past 18 years, OCE has safely sent 146 student delegations (totaling 594 participants) overseas and hosted 34 student delegations (totaling 378 participants) from abroad. The trip will last from December 28th- January 3rd. If you decide to participate, you will join a global community of over 900 OCE alumni.*

Is it just a coincidence that the trip would start on my supposed birthday? We've always celebrated my birthday on December 28th even though we don't know when I was actually born. The letter continues with more details about travel itinerary and cost. It's actually kind of expensive, but luckily there are fundraising options.

Hopefully, I can convince my parents to let me go. I never thought I would be returning to my birthplace. Literally, swimming will be my ticket there. I walk downstairs as my parents are cooking breakfast.

"So, can I go?"

"We'll need to talk this over and work out all of the details..." She places two slices of sourdough bread in the toaster.

"But...?"

"It sounds like a legitimate trip. You have been working hard all season. But are you sure you want to go on your birthday?" My dad takes a bite of his scrambled eggs.

"Yes. I feel like this is something that I need to do... And I want to go."

"Okay, we'll keep thinking about it. You'll need to figure out how to pay for the trip," my mom says.

"How about we talk tonight." My dad finishes his eggs and hugs me before leaving for work.

I go back upstairs to change and get ready for school. Now that the high school swim season is over, I don't have morning swims anymore. I will still have my afternoon practices for my club team, but at least my mornings can be a little more relaxed.

~

When I get to school, I see Kate and rush over. "Will your family let you go?" I ask.

"I hope so."

"I think we need to let the OCE know by December if we're going."

"I just don't know about the whole money thing right now. I think it would be a lot to ask of Richard and David."

"Well, we can definitely fundraise together, if that helps."

"I think it would, thanks. Hey, were you born in Guangzhou?"

"Yeah. I'm a little nervous about going back. I don't know

what it'll be like...I don't know what to expect."

"That's understandable."

"You know, when I was younger, I used to dream about finding my birth parents. I know it's so unlikely, but..."

"—I get it. If you ever want to talk about it, let me know. I mean you've been helping me. Remember that day after morning swim?"

"Yeah."

"Well, I felt a lot better after talking to you."

~

At dinner, I ask the question I've been holding in all day.

"Can I go?"

There's a noticeable pause at the table. Charlotte reaches over me for another helping of eggplant parmesan.

"We have something we need to tell you." My mom's pushing her food around her plate.

"Okay, what?"

"Yes, you can go to China..." My dad doesn't sound too happy about it.

"—Thank you!" I exclaim.

"But there's something else we need to tell you. As we were gathering all your paperwork for your Chinese visa, we ran into a little difficulty. Do you remember that day you saw Huī Yīn written on your picture?" My mom takes a sip of water.

"Yeah, you didn't want to talk about it."

"Right, we weren't sure when it would be appropriate to tell you this," she continues.

"It wasn't something we wanted to worry you with." My dad sighs.

Charlotte interjects, "Okay, what's going on? I'm confused."

I breathe in, afraid of what I might hear. I don't know why I am so afraid. Something in my gut just feels wrong.

My mom takes a deep breath, "When you were adopted, we think you were switched with another girl in the orphanage."

"I was switched? Why?" My hand starts to tremble and my

voice shakes.

"It's hard to explain. We don't know. When we were first starting the process of adopting, we were sent baby pictures of you, but another name was on them. Not Yìng Yuè, but Huī Yīn," explains my dad.

"I don't understand."

"I know honey, we're trying to explain." My mom shifts in her chair. "In China, the interpreter told us there had been some sort of mix up or switch with you and Huī Yīn. Apparently, the orphanage wanted to keep Huī Yīn for further observations. They thought maybe she had a disability. So instead, the orphanage decided that you needed to find a home sooner. You were not doing well there. They thought that you should take her place and that's all we know."

"Why are you telling me all this now?"

My dad clears his throat. "Well, with the visa paperwork there is a discrepancy between your birthday that we celebrate and the one on your passport. The passport birthday is Huī Yīn's birthday that you had to keep when we adopted you. The birthday we celebrate is the one that the pediatrician thought was closer to your actual birthday."

"Oh. I found that passport with the other documents. I was going to ask you about it... I couldn't understand why those two birthdays were different." I guess it was beginning to make sense.

"We think it's because during the switch, the orphanage gave you Huī Yīn's birthday and name. In order to continue with your adoption, you assumed Huī Yīn's identity. All of the switching had already happened by the time we arrived to formally adopt you. At the time we didn't understand what had happened to Huī Yīn. We knew we wanted to adopt you and that's what we did." My mom looks like she's about to start crying.

"Why didn't you tell me all of this sooner? And why didn't you do anything to help Huī Yīn? Didn't you think it was weird what was going on?" I ask, shocked. I can't wrap my head around it.

Throughout all of this, Charlotte looks like she is trying to understand.

"So, you're saying Leila was switched with another girl? And you never met the other girl? Do you know what happened to her?" she asks.

"Unfortunately, the orphanage never explained it. And we weren't able to ask," my mom responds.

"We didn't realize what was going on until everything had already happened. It was too late. We had you. We didn't tell you sooner because we didn't know when it would be the right time. To this day, we don't know why the switch took place." My dad now looks like he's getting choked up.

"This is a lot," I say slowly.

I take a deep breath and excuse myself. I carry my dishes to the sink and walk up the stairs to my room. Great, more things to fill my head. As if just returning to China wasn't enough. My life and adoption story are getting more and more complicated.

What does all of this mean? Who is Huī Yīn? Where is she? Is she still at the orphanage? Does she know about the switch?

I can't stop thinking about my potential China trip. What if I meet my birth parents? What if someone remembers me from when I was at the orphanage? What if I remember something? So many what ifs.

I'm excited; I'm nervous; I feel a little scared. Could I find answers? Maybe I could track down Huī Yīn. I'd had so much swimming on my mind that I'd *almost* forgotten about the name and the birthday.

"Charlotte, are you awake?" I whisper.

She's probably already asleep. My clock reads 11:57 p.m.

"Uh huh...?" she says groggily.

"What do you think about the switch?"

"It's unreal."

"I know, I can't stop thinking about Huī Yīn. I wonder what happened to her."

"Do you still want to go to China?"

"Yeah. I think so."

"What if you find Huī Yīn or meet your birth parents?"

"I know, I already thought of that. Do you think they would remember me? Do you think they would recognize me? I have so many questions for them."

"Leila, of course they would remember you. You were their daughter that they had to give up."

"But what if I don't find them? What if I don't remember anything?"

"Leila, I'm so tired. Can we talk in the morning?"

"Sure, thanks Char. See you tomorrow."

Questions and thoughts continue to swirl around in my head. I get up around one a.m. and start jotting down some of my thoughts. The China trip has sparked so many unanswered questions about my adoption. Maybe writing can be an outlet for all of my wonderings. I write a letter to my birth parents, even though I know I will never send it and probably never see them.

Dear birth Mom and Dad,

I want you to know that I am doing well. I have a loving family and a sister who is not related to me by blood, but we love each other just the same. I am a competitive swimmer and enjoy baking.

I was recently invited to swim in Guangzhou. Preparing for the trip has me thinking about questions I never knew I had. I thought writing you this letter might help me release some of the thoughts that are on my mind.

Here we go.

Why did you give me up for adoption?

What is my birthday?

What did you name me?

Do I have any siblings?

What do you look like?

Do you remember me?

Do you want to find me?

If things were different, would you have kept me?

I know that you probably wanted the best for me, but I can't help wondering and thinking about what ifs. What would my life have been like if I had lived in China with you?

I want you to know that I understand.

I hope someday I can meet you.

I don't know how to sign off. Love Leila?

Leila is my American name. My name in the orphanage was Yìng Yuè, but my birth parents wouldn't know that either. Who am I to them? A name is something so small, so ordinary, but also so full of meaning... Eventually, I drift off to sleep... I dream of a crying baby...

Chapter 16

Yìng Yuè (Leila)

In my dream, my birth mother sees me for the first time. She doesn't know how to express her love for me. I see her wrapping me in a blanket and singing me to sleep as I snuggle close to her for warmth. I think, today is a good day to be alive.

As I am sleeping, my mother rocks me, and the rest of my birth family takes turns visiting us. My mother quietly tells my dad and her parents to be quiet so as not to wake me. I hear them talking about how pale my skin is and how tiny I am. I wish they wouldn't focus so much on my appearance, because I know deep down that I am just fine. There is nothing to be worried about.

My mother falls asleep, and that's when I decide I am done sleeping. I make noises and try to wiggle around. My grandmother sees me struggling and lifts me out of my birth mother's arms. She looks at me, and I look at her. I don't know what to make of her deep brown eyes that are narrowed into slits. She reminds me of a snake analyzing its prey, deciding if it's worth the chase.

I'm scared and want to cry out, but then her whole demeanor changes. She smiles at me and sings the same lullaby my mother sang to me earlier. My father walks in and smiles as well. He takes me from her, and I feel at ease in his arms. I trust him.

My father begins to cry because he knows that he can't

keep me. He knows that China's one-child policy will make it impossible to keep me. They can't afford to have a second child. My mother wakes up and sees me in my father's arms.

She asks, "But why not? Why can't we keep her?"

"You know why," my father replies.

A week passes and my mother is feeding me. She can't take her eyes off me, and in the background, I hear my older brother playing with our grandparents. It sounds like they're playing with a ball. Maybe it's that game where they hit the ball against the wall. If I were older, I think I would like to play.

My mother sighs and starts to cry. This time my father comforts her.

He says, "Just one more week, and then it must be done."

A month goes by, and I am still with my family. My grandparents have distanced themselves from me and hardly touch me. I don't mind because I know my mother loves me. She always starts the day singing my favorite lullaby and lifting me into the air as she washes me. This is my favorite part of the day. We are happiest in the morning. Some days we go outside and smell the fresh air, but usually we stay inside away from prying eyes.

Three more months have passed, and today I hear my grandmother arguing with my mother. My grandmother is worried about the family. She's telling my mother that if she doesn't do it, then she and the rest of the family are leaving. They won't risk the chance of someone finding out that I'm still here. She is begging my mother to think about everyone else.

"Don't you realize you are putting your family in danger?" my grandmother shouts.

"Yìng Yuè is part of the family." She holds me tightly in her arms.

"Yìng Yuè is still so young. She will be okay. You need to do it for yourself and for her. If you wait longer it'll be worse," my grandmother says in a solemn tone.

"What if they never find out?" counters my mother.

"That's impossible. The neighbors are already wondering. The news is going to get out and once it does, it will spread."

"I just can't do it. I won't do it."

"It's your grave you're digging."

It's been almost nine months since my birth. My brother is taking care of me while my parents are visiting my grandparents. My grandparents moved away after the last fight with my mother about me.

Sadly, they won't let my parents bring me to visit them, which is why my eight-year-old brother is looking after me. My brother is quiet. He mostly just stares at me with curiosity. We don't see each other much, since he's usually gone all day at school. Today, he seems more interested in me and wants to play peek-a-boo. I laugh at him as he makes the silly faces.

I hear the slam of doors as my mom rushes in and holds me close. My father yells something at her and tries to pull me out of her arms. She doesn't let go, and I can feel her nervous energy. I'm scared. I don't understand what is happening.

Another month goes by. I am ten months old. I should be excited to have made it to this age, but I can tell that something isn't right. My mother is gone, and my father has a sad look in his eyes. He lifts me out of my crib and wraps me in a blanket. It's different from the one I usually sleep in. It feels new and kind of scratchy. I hear my father trying to talk to me, but his voice cracks. Before I know it, I am laid in a basket and covered with a blanket. I am left on a doorstep.

Chapter 17

Yìng Yuè (Leila)

Was I dreaming of my past or just a possible reality? My mind must have been trying to make sense of my unanswered questions. I don't know if dreaming about the possibilities helped, or if not really knowing the truth just made it worse.

Another day of the usual routine. It's all kind of a blur. I'm not thinking; I'm simply going through the motions. I'm still struggling to come to terms with what happened. What does all of this mean? Who is Huī Yīn? Is she still at the orphanage? Does she know about the switch?

~

That night I have another dream. I dream that I am Huī Yīn.

My birth was quick. I never knew the touch of my mother. I took my first breath, and I was swaddled in blankets and left on a bench at the train station. I was found in the morning and taken to the White Cloud Orphanage. There, the volunteers bathed and clothed me. I was rocked to sleep. I didn't cry. I didn't make a sound. I was in shock.

One month later, I am lying in the orphanage crib. I look up at the ceiling and see streaks of paint and dirt mixed together. I am a quiet baby. I know only this room. I see other babies like myself. We are all lying in our identical cribs. We take comfort in each other. We know that we aren't truly alone; we have each other.

I'm five months old. The volunteers and nannies are reading to the babies in the nursery. One is brushing my short hair. I love the sound of their voices. It makes me feel special when Daina comes over and holds me for a few minutes before she has to move on to the next baby. She puts me back in my crib; I feel suddenly cold. Time continues. I feel nothing.

I am almost a year old. I have overcome great adversity to make it to this age. The nannies are surprised that I am still alive. Many thought I would be one of the unlucky ones by now, all except Daina.

Daina knew how special I was, and she showed me what love could feel like. I miss her. She had to go back home, and I don't know if I'll ever see her again.

Today is my birthday. I just turned one. Birthdays in the orphanage are not celebrated because no one knows when anyone's birthday is. We don't get presents; we don't sing. Sometimes if we're lucky, we might get an extra sweet or maybe extra time with one of the nannies.

I should be babbling, but I am not. I don't know why. My voice doesn't want to work. I was never a crier, and everyone always wondered why. Is something wrong with me? I envy the kids that can move on their own. I long to get out of my crib and try taking my first step. Instead, I am stuck behind these bars of mine. I can't move, I can't talk. I'm stuck in my head.

I wake up sobbing today. I can't help feeling a whole rush of emotions as I think about Huī Yīn and the life she might have had. I feel so guilty for taking her place. What would her life have been like if she had been adopted instead of me? Does she hate me?

My birthday, or my celebrated birthday, is approaching. After learning about Huī Yīn, I don't know how to feel. I put on a brave face, and I try to act like everything is normal. I don't want people to feel sorry for me or make me feel even more different than I already am. I need to focus on school and swimming. After all, swimming is what got me into this confusion and hopefully it can get me out of it.

At the pool, I am pushing myself harder than usual. Breaks are pointless, I don't need them. I don't want to stop. Swimming is all that there is. I don't feel the burning of my lungs not getting enough air. I don't feel the stiffness of my muscles cramping up. My coach whistles for me to stop, but I don't; I can't. I keep going and going until I can go no more.

When I finally stop, everyone is gone. I guess practice finished a long time ago. My coach is still there waiting for me. He waits for me to start talking on my own terms.

It all rushes out. He listens. I feel empty, emotionally and physically. I think I tried to bottle everything up for too long. Sooner or later it was going to be overwhelming. I feel like a weight is starting to lift off my chest.

He pats my shoulder. "Leila, I am always here to listen if you need someone to talk to, but I think maybe you should talk to your parents. Or if you wanted to talk to a school counselor, I could help with that."

"Thanks Coach. Sorry about practice today. I guess it was my way of working through everything."

"I understand. Let's just try not to make a habit of it. If something is bothering you, sometimes it's best to talk to someone like you did today."

"Okay. See you tomorrow."

I walk into the locker room and take my time. I'm still processing. I think what Coach said is true. Talking about my problems isn't my style. I usually try not to get overly emotional, but today, sharing has seemed to help. That night, I dream again. This time it's me as a baby.

Yìng Yuè

I slept outside all night and caught a cold. I was found in the morning. The volunteers at the orphanage thought I wouldn't make it through the week. Surely, my body would give out. But my body was stronger than it looked. I fought for my life and within a week, I was as healthy as I had ever been.

I cry nonstop, longing for the warmth of my mother. I miss her singing and her love. I don't understand where I am. I miss my silly brother who I was just beginning to know. Where did they go? Why are these strangers feeding me?

I'm crying again. The volunteers are tired of me. They have moved me to the older kids' floor. I am told to be quiet. I am told to stop crying. I cry anyway. I can't help it. I want my mother. I need my mother.

Gradually, I stop crying as much. The volunteers whisper about how unhappy I look. (Don't all children at orphanages look unhappy?) One day, I hear one of the volunteers say, "She's getting worse."

I didn't notice it at first, but I have started to feel more withdrawn from the rest of the children. I used to eat my meals at the table with the older kids, but now the food doesn't interest me anymore. I don't even want to eat my favorite rice bowl.

Weeks go by, and I have lost a lot of weight. I no longer want people to touch or hold me. I am sad and weak. My skin is sickly. "She's too pale," I hear someone say.

The orphanage nurse stopped by to see me and said something about a "failure to thrive syndrome." I don't know what she is talking about and I don't care. I just feel like the world could go on without me and I would just slip away unnoticed...

It's weird—all of this feels so real, and I don't know the difference between dreams and reality anymore. Did that actually happen, or is my mind trying to piece together what little information I know and create a new memory?

My birthday will be here soon. I will turn fifteen the day I fly to China. But, if my birthday isn't my actual birthday, does it still matter? Ugh, I don't know anymore.

I try to enjoy myself, and I am happy to be with my friends and family, but I can't help thinking of Huī Yīn today. What is she doing right now? What is going through her mind? Before I know it, the day has turned to night, and in my sleep I dream.

Huī Yīn

Maybe there is something wrong with me. I don't know. Some days I feel more interested in what is happening around me than others. I used to hear this crying baby all of the time, and it got annoying. But now I don't hear her as much. I wonder what happened.

Today, I figure out which baby was the one who was crying so much. She looks a little younger than me and has extremely pale skin. I wonder if something is wrong with her. She is now a lot quieter than most of the other younger babies. She looks sick.

The volunteers take everyone except for her to eat breakfast together. There are five of us who are over a year, but under two years. We all eat in silence. We don't expect much. We're used to the silence, to being alone.

I'm almost two years old, but I still can't walk. I don't know what's wrong with me. It's like my mind knows what to do, but my body won't do it. I feel like I'm stuck. I see some of the other girls walking or at least crawling. I'm still having trouble just sitting up. What is wrong with me?

"Do you think she'll make it?" The nanny with glasses is at it again. Why all the questions?

"She's developing so slowly," the kind red butterfly woman says.

"Should we move her to the other room?"

"Don't say that! Give her another week."

The baby who was always crying is starting to stand and is trying to walk on her own. She looks at me. I look at her. We share a brief moment together, and then it's gone. She is taken away, and I don't see her again.

These dreams are harder and harder to take. It's painful to try to think about Huī Yīn, yet at the same time, I can't stop. There's this need within me to know what happened. December 28th is getting closer every day, which means soon I will be traveling to China with the swim group. What's going to happen when I get there? What will I feel?

The last day before break, everyone in Mrs. Demore's class presents their family history projects. Everyone except me. I am able to get an extension until after break because of the trip. I promise that when I return, I will send her an updated version of my project, and we will go from there.

~

Winter break starts, and I don't see much of Jasmine or Kate. Jasmine and her mom go to a ski resort in Canada every year, and Kate seems busy partaking in new holiday traditions with the Michaelsons. We still have our group text going, but I wish I could see them in person. Two days before the flight, Jasmine sends a group text.

Are you ready for China? It's so soon!

I know, I text back. I have so many emotions going through me, I'm not sure what to say.

Yes, I can't wait! replies Kate.

Jasmine asks, *@Leila Are you ready for everything? You've been dealing with a lot lately.*

I hope so, I respond.

When I told them about the switch, they were very supportive. It's nice being able to confide in them. Charlotte tries to understand, but she's younger, and it's not the same.

We're here if you want to talk, texts Kate.

And you were always there when we were going through all our drama, texts Jasmine.

Thank you. I send a smiley face and heart then turn off my phone.

That night, I fall asleep looking through my old baby photos, and Huī Yīn returns.

Chapter 18

Yìng Yuè (Leila)

"Why wasn't Huī Yīn adopted?" the volunteer with red butterflies on her shirt asks.

"She was switched," the nanny with glasses responds.

"Why? Who decided that?"

"I don't know. They wanted to observe her. They thought she might have a disability."

Someone enters the room. He clears his throat.

"She's just developing slowly due to severe neglect. She needs more personal, one-on-one interactions with her caregivers," the man in a white coat says.

"But she hasn't even spoken yet. Is that normal?" The red butterfly woman picks me up.

"No, of course not, but given her circumstances, it should be expected that she'll have mental, emotional, and physical delays. Her development is slow, but I think she'll be okay."

I believe that kind doctor. I will be okay. I am okay. There's nothing wrong with me; my body is just taking its time. I believe in me, too.

In the morning, the volunteer comes by to check on me and says her usual, "Good morning Huī Yīn."

"G-GG-o-oo moo"

"What was that?"

I smile; I have done it! My voice does work. The volunteer comes back to visit me later that day. She plays with me, and I laugh. I think it is my first laugh in a long time.

A few weeks later, I notice my clothes tightening around my body. They are constricting my movement, and the volunteer notices it too. She brings me bigger clothes and helps me put them on. I stretch. I can reach up! My arms don't go very high, but I can move them! The volunteer smiles. I think she believes in me too.

I wake. Well, at least in my mind Huī Yīn has a couple of kind people who care for her. Tomorrow I fly to China. I can't believe how fast all of this has come together. I think of Huī Yīn constantly and wonder if I might be able to visit my orphanage. I wonder if she is still there. What has become of her? What is her life like?

Chapter 19

Yìng Yuè (Leila)

Happy Birthday.

I don't feel any different. I guess I'm a year older. But am I really?

I walk downstairs and smell my favorite breakfast cooking. The waffle iron beeps. Mm, warm buttery waffles fresh off the iron. My mom pours her homemade tangy blueberry sauce into the elephant-shaped syrup holder while my dad is furiously whisking the cream.

I sit down at the dining room table and cue the singing.

"Happy Birthday to you, Happy Birthday to you,
Happy Birthday, dear Leila,
Happy Birthday to you!"

No one can ever sing that in tune, can they?

Charlotte hands me a plate. I pile on two waffles, blueberry sauce, and a dollop of whipped cream. My mom sticks a candle in the whipped cream and lights it. They say, "Happy Birthday!" one more time, and I blow out the candle.

"I have something for you." Charlotte gives me a small red envelope with a cute dog on the front of it.

It's a Chinese tradition to give hóngbāo (red envelopes) on or around Chinese New Year. Even though it's December, it's still technically the year of the dog. Today, she thinks it'll bring me luck for my long trip ahead.

I peel open the envelope, and inside is a thick stack of colorful Chinese rénmínbì.

This money makes the trip feel so real, but I still can't believe I'll be flying to China in a few short hours.

While Mom and Dad are cleaning up, Charlotte helps me check my bags one more time. We go through my list.

"Toothbrush, toothpaste, brush, charger, swimsuit, cap, goggles..."

"Yes, I have all that."

"Phone, passport, money?"

"Check."

"I think that's everything! Oh wait, one more thing." She hands me a pair of brand-new memory foam slippers. "In case there's a cold wood floor in the hotel."

"Thanks, Char."

~

When we arrive at the Portland International Airport, I open the trunk and pull out my black swim bag and red carry-on suitcase. I've remembered to tie the OCE yellow ribbons and blue ID tags on my luggage to help with identification should something happen to them.

My family walks with me as far as they can before I have to go through security. I notice my parents' eyes getting watery.

"Don't cry." I hand them my travel sized pouch of generic tissues. I knew these would come in handy. I didn't realize it would be so soon.

"We're going to miss you, but we hope you find what you're looking for." My mom dabs her eyes with a tissue.

I give everyone a quick hug; I'm as ready as I'll ever be.

"Bring me back something cool!" calls Charlotte as I walk toward security. Oh, Charlotte, I smile.

I'm looking for Kate and see her standing next to the giant

reader board. There's our flight, CA154. It reads, On time.

We make our way to the gate and introduce ourselves to the rest of the group. All of the swimmers placed in the top three for their individual or relay events. The coaches have volunteered from various teams throughout Oregon. While we're waiting for the last few swimmers to show up, people are chatting among themselves.

I'm quiet. I'm not sure how to feel. My mind is distant. Can Huī Yīn sense that I'm headed her way?

Kate pokes my shoulder. "Hey, are you okay?"

"Yeah, I'm just taking it all in."

"Yeah, I get it. Do you want to talk?"

I shake my head.

"Make sure you have your boarding pass and passport out. Let's get in line," Marcy, our group leader says.

I close my eyes and inhale deeply. I can do this.

~

"Welcome aboard. We'll be taking off shortly," announces the captain through the audio system.

I walk behind Kate and let some people go by. Then I reach up to put my red carry-on in the overhead compartment. Kate lets me take the window seat, so I climb over her. The TV screens in the seats in front of us start to play the routine safety video while the flight attendants demonstrate the procedures.

I feel the plane picking up speed as we're gaining momentum down the runway. The flight attendants sit down, and their seat belts click into place. Then I notice the all-too-familiar feeling of losing gravity as the plane lifts off the ground. My ears pop. I try to get as comfy as I can because it's going to be a long 18-hour flight.

As I'm starting to doze off, I think about how grateful I am for Kate and Jasmine's friendship. Even though Jasmine won't be with us physically, she's promised to check in through WeChat, which is how we can get around international texting.

Fortunately, Kate will be with me. She'll be my rock as I go through one of the most emotional journeys of my life. I'm about to come to terms with my life in the orphanage. I'm returning to my place of birth. I may be able to find answers to my questions, or I may not. Who knows? Now, it's just the Pacific Ocean between me and my future...or my past?

I don't remember what I had been dreaming about before I'm jolted awake. Lightning strikes right outside our window.

"It's just a little turbulence. Please remain seated, and fasten your seatbelts." The captain remains calm and navigates us around a slightly frightening thunderstorm.

Three hours later, we land safely in China. "Welcome to Guangzhou, the local time is 14:05. The temperature is a balmy 22 degrees Celsius. Thank you for flying with Air China."

I step off the plane and feel the dry air on my skin. It's not as smoggy as I heard it would be. Well, that's good at least. I look around the landing area. I can't see much of the city yet. We're mostly surrounded by other airplanes that have landed or are waiting to take off.

A shiver runs down my shoulders and back. You know that feeling when your skin feels tingly? When you feel like something is about to happen, but you don't know what? I feel like something big is coming.

After we get through customs, Marcy makes a quick phone call and then leads us to where a charter bus is waiting.

It'll be a short, but hopefully rewarding trip. Before I left, my parents worked with Marcy to arrange for an interpreter to help me visit my orphanage on the final free day. It seemed like a perfect opportunity, and I didn't want to pass it up. I wish I could skip to the end.

On the bus ride, I think about our meet against the provincial team. I wonder how fast they are. Will we have a chance, or will they easily beat us? How much do they train? I know with some sports schools you have to live in a training facility. Do these Chinese swimmers live at school?

It takes nearly an hour to get to the China Hotel due to all the traffic and congestion. Finally, the bus drops us off. The sign has five brightly-lit stars under the large letters of the name.

As we walk through the automatic doors, someone is playing on a shiny grand piano, and chandeliers glisten overhead. The lobby is huge and includes a 7-11, a jewelry counter, and souvenir stalls. It's so long that there's a moving sidewalk!

I stick close to Kate, and we're handed our room key.

"We will leave for dinner at six, meet here in the lobby." Marcy points to the lounge area, and everyone disperses.

Kate and I are staying in room 1101. How many floors does this hotel have? This isn't even the tallest building in the city. I read that Canton Tower holds that record. It was the tallest building in the world between 2009-2011.

We ride the elevator up to the 11th floor and walk down the hall to our room. I unlock the door, and inside we see two queen sized beds, a couch, flatscreen TV, and a bathroom with a walk-in shower. Kate immediately starts unpacking and organizing her swim stuff.

I take my shoes off and hop onto one of the queen beds. I probably should take a shower after all that traveling, but I'm so tired, I could pass out.

As Kate is folding her clothes, I ask, "Can you go with me to the orphanage?"

"Of course!" She acts like it is a no-brainer.

"Thanks. I don't know if I could do that on my own." My anxiety starts to lessen just a little.

It's nearly six. Kate and I change out of our stinky airplane clothes. During the bus ride to the hotel, Marcy was going on and on about the Peking duck she pre-ordered for us. Even though it's typically from northern China, and we're in the southern part, it's a Chinese specialty that Marcy insists we try. I've never had duck before; I wonder if it's like chicken.

We eat dinner at the White Flower which has been around since 1935. At least, that's what I think our tour guide said. It's an old, two-story building with more than 20 dining rooms for large and small groups. In the center is a tropical garden and a lush pond with seating around it.

Our group follows the waitress up an elegant staircase to the second floor. The room has stained glass windows on one side; the other looks out to some lanterns and a tree that grows up from the garden below.

We're seated at a long oval table. Already on the table are two white porcelain teapots filled with black tea. I spin the lazy Susan to bring the tea closer to me and pour myself a cup. It's surprisingly sweet and fragrant.

Everyone is given a small bowl of white rice, and we share a plate of sautéed bamboo shoots, lotus roots, mushrooms, snap peas, and bok choy. Steamed fish with garlic and ginger in a seafood broth is placed to the right of me. I'm not a huge fan of fish, but I try it anyway, and it's not bad.

The star of the show is the Peking duck. It was gently roasted for hours and served with its crispy skin. When the duck comes to me, I use my chopsticks to place a few bites on my plate. It's good, but my favorite dish of the night is the soup dumplings. The savory broth with a pork and green onion filling melt in my mouth. I could easily eat a full plate of them on my own. For dessert, we each receive a small bowl of silky-smooth milk custard topped with red beans.

Mm... I almost feel like eating the local cuisine is bringing back distant memories. A déjà vu sort of remembrance. But that couldn't be, could it?

Chapter 20

Yìng Yuè (Leila)

At seven a.m., there's a sharp knock on our door. It's Marcy's version of an alarm.

I turn over and reach for the light switch. I slowly roll out of bed and start collecting my swim gear for today.

"No... Can I have five more minutes?" Kate tries to cover her head.

"I think we should get ready. We still need time to eat and then meet everyone down in the lobby."

She groggily gets up and stretches.

We're both still feeling jet lagged, but maybe eating some breakfast will help. As we step into the buffet room, we're greeted with trays and trays of fresh fruit, ranging from dark purple dragon fruit to bright orange passion fruit along with rounds of pineapple and sliced mango. The two tables in the middle of the room are divided into Chinese and Western-style breakfast options.

The smells coming from the food make my stomach growl. I wish I could try everything, but with swim practice in less than an hour, I maintain self-control. I pick up a plate and use the tongs to pick up a freshly steamed pork bun and some dragon fruit. I carry my food to the table, and then go back to pour a glass of the sweet and slightly tart mango-orange juice.

From our table, I can see Canton Tower in the distance. On the street below us, people are already busy getting ready for the day. Cars, buses, taxis, and bicycles are loaded with passengers. School children are walking around in their uniforms. Families stop by local shops to pick up breakfast. This was once my home. I wonder who I would be today if I had stayed here.

~

"This is where the Guangzhou provincial swim team trains and lives." Marcy is reading off the Guangzhou School of Sport brochure. "Some of their students have gone on to be World and Olympic champions."

"Are we meeting the swimmers today?" Kate asks.

"Unfortunately, they're busy, but the director will give us a tour. We'll get to see a martial arts performance and watch the badminton athletes after practice."

~

Practice is not what I expected. First off, this new pool is a 50-meter pool. That means for my event, the 50 free, there is no wall to do a flip turn. I'm used to using the wall to build up more speed, so not having one makes me feel much slower. Second, endurance-wise, 50 meters may not seem like that much longer than 50 yards, but it is. I'll have to get used to this distance in time for our little meet. On the other hand, I guess this is the kind of pool they use in the Olympics...

Kate and I learn that we'll be on a relay with Annie from Salem and Calla from Bend. In the medley, Kate will swim backstroke, Annie breaststroke, Calla butterfly, and I'll do freestyle. Maybe this is my redemption race for missing out on the State medley relay.

Since we all placed in the top three at State in our respective events, we should make up a pretty fast team. We might even have a chance at winning. The nice thing is that there's no pressure. This trip is focused on learning about Chinese culture and meeting local students. I wonder what Huī Yīn is doing now. Is she at school? Does she like to swim? What if she ended up here, at this school? I might never know.

After practice, a local tour guide shows us around some of the city's historical museums and landmarks. The Chen Clan Ancestral Hall's roof is decorated with intricate wooden carvings. This famous architecture is from the Qing dynasty. I don't know much about all the Chinese dynasties, but I do know the Qing dynasty was the last dynasty in China.

Inside, older women try to show us how to do traditional paper cutting. I trace chūn, the Chinese character for spring and carefully cut around it. Kate attempts to cut out her character, fú for good luck.

"On Chinese New Year, or the Spring Festival, chūn and fú are hung upside down on doors to welcome in spring and bring good fortune," our guide says.

Even though it's not springtime yet, maybe our chūn and fú will bring me luck while I'm here. I still have the red envelope with money my family gave me.

We get back on the bus, and I'm half listening to the guide talk about Guāngxiào Temple. I'm thinking about Huī Yīn and the orphanage. While it's nearly impossible to learn about my birth parents, finding Huī Yīn, or at least finding out what happened to her, might not be so impossible.

"We're here," Kate whispers and nudges me.

I didn't realize I'd fallen asleep. I look out the window and see a magnificent entrance. There are two stone lion statues guarding the front gate, and gold Chinese characters are written across the front and side panels. Due to my limited Mandarin, I'm not completely sure what it says. But I think it is something along the lines of "Guāngxiào Temple, Buddhist school and temple."

The smoky incense draws Kate and me to the giant Buddha where half a dozen people are kneeling. Around us, more people are leaving offerings; others are adding incense to the little pots set out around the chamber.

I'm not spiritual, but standing here among people who look like me and could very well be my distant relatives, I feel connected to this place. Do my birth parents practice

Buddhism? Could they be among the locals visiting the temple today?

It's a quick stop—soon we're led away to the Five Goats Statue.

"The statue is from the Legend of Five Goats. In a time of drought and famine, five gods rode in on five goats," our guide explains. "The gods left behind grain and the goats. People planted the grain and from then on, they had rich harvests and rains. Guangzhou now has the name 'City of Five Goats.'"

Everywhere we go is packed with people. It seems the locals are always on the move. As we pass through different parts of the city, there's a sharp contrast in housing. I see people living in crumbling buildings with all their clothing hanging outside to dry. Just a few doors down, I see tall, state of the art skyscrapers with pristine glass windows.

I wonder where I would have lived. Do my parents live and work in the city? Maybe they work in the countryside as farmers. Would I have gone to school? Or would I have had to stay at home take care of siblings? Would I have been happy?

That night, we have a quiet dinner at the Huáměi International School with some high school students. They've been studying English since first grade, and they're full of questions.

"Where are you from? Do you like China?" one of the students asks.

"We're from Oregon. It's a state on the west coast of the US." Kate points to a map on her phone.

"I love the food here," I say as I shovel noodles into my mouth. My chopstick skills are improving.

"Do you speak Chinese? Are you Chinese?" a different student asks me.

I nod. "Yes, I speak a little Chinese. I was adopted from Guangzhou."

"Oh. Are your parents Chinese?" They look confused.

"No, I was adopted by white parents. I don't look like them." I try to explain. They are having a hard time understanding what it means to be adopted. I try again, this time in Chinese. "Wǒ bèi lǐngyǎng de."

Saying it in Chinese seems to help. I watch as realization crosses their faces. I show them pictures of my family and our high school.

"Do you live there?" someone asks.

"No, we just go during the day. Kate and I swim on our high school's team." Kate shows a picture of us at State.

Before we say goodbye, I give the Huáměi students Oregon-shaped keychains with Mount Hood on them. Kate and I had to look all over Portland to find the perfect local souvenir that wouldn't be too heavy. In return, the students give us little boxes of origami cranes, each the size of my fingernail and Chinese stationery.

Chapter 21

Yìng Yuè (Leila)

Today, we don't have practice until the afternoon, so I decide to splurge and try the dim sum for breakfast. I look at all the little baskets filled with their bite-sized goodies. By the time we are done eating, I feel like my stomach is about to burst.

A little later, a small group of us decide to go to Báiyún Mountain, also known as White Cloud Mountain. I wonder if I was named after something related to the mountain. My Chinese name is Yìng Yuè. It means "reflection of the moon." Now that I think about it, the moon's in the sky like clouds, and a moon's reflection could be considered cloud-like. Could that be where my name comes from?

The hotel helps us hire a taxi so we can be dropped off at the Báiyún ticket office. As we are waiting in line to buy the tickets for the cable car up the mountain, Kate asks, "It's safe, right?"

I didn't realize she was afraid of heights.

"Hey, if you don't want to ride the cable car, we can walk," I say.

"I don't want you to miss out on it though... And it's a long hike up—" She pauses. "I think I can do it. Let's just not get one with a glass floor."

"Deal!"

When we make it to the front of the line, I step into the

cable car first. It dips slightly as I sit down. Kate holds her breath.

"You can do it." I hold open the door for her.

She ducks her head and quickly sits down across from me. We look out the windows and watch in awe as we slowly make our way to the top. Kate has one eye closed and periodically glances out before sitting as still as she can so as not to rock the car. I feel bad, but she insisted she wanted to try it. I see Guangzhou getting smaller and smaller beneath us.

All around, I hear what sounds like hundreds of birds chatting away in the trees. Soon we can make out just the tops of temples among the leafy coverage below us. We're up so high it feels like we are in the clouds. The car stops long enough for everyone to jump out, and then it starts its descent back down the mountain.

Kate looks okay; she is shaking slightly but manages to smile. I take out my phone to document the beautiful peak. As I'm taking a panorama, an orange and black butterfly flies right past my ear, and I watch it through my camera. It lands on a sign for the trail down the mountain. I guess that is our sign to make our way back.

~

After a short practice, we take the bus to the Guangdong Museum of Art. From the outside, you can tell it's an art museum. The building looks like a traditional Cantonese ivory puzzle ball. Inside, there are all kinds of art exhibitions from ceramic figures and pottery to calligraphy. Throughout this trip, I am starting to feel even more connected to this amazing city. This is my heritage, my ancestry.

"What's for dinner?" I ask Kate. The food here is so good that I can't stop thinking about what we might try next.

She takes out the schedule. "Hot pot?"

Our group fills the tiny hot pot restaurant. There is a large pot in the center of each table that is meant to be shared by four people. After we are seated, a waiter comes to turn it on. Soon, the spicy broth is boiling away, and our assortment of sliced meats, veggies, noodles and other add-ins arrive on large platters. We are instructed to use one set of chopsticks to put the raw food in the broth, and another pair to eat with.

I gently drop some tofu and mushrooms into the broth. Kate adds an egg and noodles. Calla chooses some thinly sliced beef, and Annie sets the sweet potatoes and chicken carefully in the pot. We watch as our items cook away, and within minutes our food is ready.

I use my clean chopsticks to pull out my tofu and mushrooms and place them on top of my bowl of rice. Before taking a bite, I dip my tofu and rice into the unique sauce. Mm, the rest of the table is pleased with their choices, and we keep adding more of everything to our broth for a second and third round.

~

Sunday is here, which means we will finally be competing in the international meet. We have a quick warm-up and then it's time for our medley relay.

"Take your mark." *Beep!*

Kate's the lead off and she's in. She's doing great and coming to the wall. She touches. Annie dives over her. Annie's breaststroke is fast and her technique is flawless. She's right there with the Chinese team. Calla's butterfly is good, but we start to fall behind a little. It's almost my turn. My adrenaline kicks in, and I hear, "Go Leila!" as I dive in.

Breathe, stroke, kick, kick, kick, stroke, kick, kick, kick repeat. It's going to be a close race. People are cheering. It's the last few meters. I'm almost there. Here it comes... I slam into the wall and...

We're all checking the board. The results flash before us. The times are within two hundredths of a second. The winner is...the Chinese provincial team. It's hard not to be disappointed, but we all did our best. For being in a new country and swimming in a different pool with meters instead of yards, I think we did well.

After the meet, both teams share an evening cruise boat down the Pearl River. It's part of the cultural exchange. From the boat, we can see Guangzhou all lit up. Buildings and apartments are glowing, making the city look almost magical. We glide under bridges and admire the curvy Canton Tower. It has rainbow flashing lights that create geometric patterns and change every few seconds. It's a night of dancing colors and a city to remember.

As soon as dinner is finished, a cultural talent show begins. Swimmers are singing and dancing and showing off their odd talents. Kate joins in. I sit back and watch. I don't talk much. I'm thinking about my birth parents. Can they feel my presence in the city? Does Huī Yīn know I'm here? Tomorrow is the big day. I will reconnect with my past. Am I ready?

Back at the hotel, I get a message from Jasmine. It must be like six a.m. there.

How's the trip? When are you going to your orphanage?

The trip has been great so far. The meet was today. We got out-touched by the Chinese team. Kate and I are going to the orphanage tomorrow. I don't know what I feel.

I hope it works out! Maybe you'll feel better in the morning.

I hope so, too. Thanks. Talk to you tomorrow.

Chapter 22

Yìng Yuè (Leila)

"Hey, are you awake?" I gently tap Kate.

"Wh..what?"

I could hardly sleep because of my apprehension for today. For me, the whole trip was leading up to this day. I am hours away from visiting my orphanage. What will it be like? Will I remember anything from my time there? When I tried searching for the orphanage online, there were no pictures. Just an address.

At breakfast, looking at all the food makes me nauseated.

"Aren't you going to eat?" Kate points toward the food.

"I don't know if I can."

"You should eat something. Fruit?"

I grab a small plate from the buffet bar and fill it with slices of dragon fruit and watermelon. Kate's right, I should eat something. I'll need my strength. I grab a small steamed pork bun too, for protein.

Kate looks over at me. I think she can sense how anxious I am, so she tries to lighten the mood.

"Last night was so much fun! I've never been on a cruise before. And the Canton Tower, it was like a light show! It reminds me of New York at night." She sighs. "What's been your favorite thing so far?"

"The cable car up White Cloud Mountain." I nibble on my bun.

"Yeah, that was fun, even though it was kind of scary. I think the swim meet was my favorite."

~

Down in the lobby I see Marcy coming toward us.

"Marcy, what's the interpreter's name?"

"Let me check." She looks at the referral paper and says, "Her name is... Amy."

Amy, a small, middle aged woman with short black hair and round blue glasses comes rushing in.

"Nǐ hǎo, nǐ hǎo, wǒ shì Amy. You must be Yìng Yuè." She looks at me.

I nod and say, "Nǐ hǎo Amy. You can call me Yìng Yuè or Leila."

"Please, forgive me. My English isn't very good. This is my first time as an interpreter."

"Oh, no problem. It's very good!" I say.

She pauses between some of her words, but her English is understandable.

Marcy looks at Amy. "The plan is to see the White Swan Hotel and then Leila's orphanage today."

"Why a hotel?" Kate looks at me.

"It was where my parents and I stayed when they adopted me. I guess it's to retrace the original journey."

"Hǎo, let's go!" Amy leads the way to the taxi which has been rented for the day.

To get to the White Swan Hotel, we drive to an area called Shāmiàn Island. There's a small bridge that we cross. It is much smaller than I thought it would be. According to Amy, the island is only about one kilometer long and less than half a kilometer wide.

From the taxi, I can see the European colonial influence. The Victorian-style architecture stands out with its tall columns and balconies, a distinct contrast from the traditional Chinese buildings we had seen throughout our stay. The driver drops us off so we can walk around before going to my orphanage.

As we walk down the paved streets, I feel like I am going back in time. The island almost feels out of place. It is so peaceful and calm compared to the busy, noisy city of Guangzhou. We walk down one of the long streets, and I'm reminded of walking through Washington Park in Portland. There are tall flowy trees and greenery swaying in the gentle breeze. Cafés and eateries have taken over the smaller buildings, and the scent of mouth-watering baked treats fills the air.

"Hey look, it's a Starbucks!" We turn to look in the direction Kate is pointing.

"Wow, I guess you can't escape them." I laugh.

After a matter of minutes, we come to the tallest building on the island. It looks like a modern skyscraper.

"This is the White Swan Hotel. Many important people have stayed here including Queen Elizabeth II," Amy says proudly.

"Wow, it's huge! I can't believe we stayed there."

"It is known for great dim sum and has a... what's that fancy food stars award?"

"Michelin stars?"

"Yes, one of the restaurants has a Michelin star."

We don't have time to go in, but I take some pictures from the outside for my parents. I'm sure they'd be interested to see how or if it's changed.

~

Amy gives the taxi driver the address of the orphanage. It's about a 45-minute drive from Shāmiàn if there's no traffic. Since the orphanage is so far outside the main area of the city, the driver isn't as familiar with the route. He uses his phone to look up the directions.

"Have you ever been to the orphanage?" I ask Amy.

"No. I'm not familiar with the orphanages."

Marcy points out the fields of crops. "Oh, look at all the rice paddies and vegetable plots!"

We look out the windows and see massive fields growing what must be different kinds of rice and vegetables. Farmers are scattered, attending to their crops. We are getting farther from the city and the roads are becoming narrower and less paved.

I imagine my parents working in the fields. Could that be them over there? The ride gets bumpier, and we come to a complete stop.

"Is this it?" Kate glances at Amy.

Amy double checks the address. "It looks like we are here."

This is where the orphanage was supposed to be according to what I found online. We walk to the end of the road. It's dusty and surrounded by fields. I don't see anything that looks like it could be an orphanage. All that is left is an abandoned building. The windows are cracked and the door has Chinese writing scrawled across it.

I'm at a loss for words. After all the buildup, I feel like I'm about to start crying. I came all this way and found nothing. I shouldn't have hoped for answers, but I let hope guide me, and this is what happened. Now it's gone. I'm trying to keep it all together.

Amy walks over to where the farmers have gathered and are now staring at us. We must look strange to them. Here we are, a group of foreigners and locals, driving in a taxi just to find an old, deserted building. Amy starts talking to the farmers in Chinese.

I can understand pieces of the conversation. She's asking if they know what happened. They shake their heads. Someone new is talking to her. Amy thanks them for their time and rejoins us.

"They think the orphanage closed down a few years ago. It moved closer to the city. We can search for the New White Cloud Orphanage," she says.

We get back in the taxi and Amy starts looking up information about the New White Cloud Orphanage. I'm trying not to get optimistic, but with this news, my hope returns. Maybe it isn't a lost cause.

"Found it!" exclaims Amy. I wait for her to continue.

"I'm going to call them right now. Okay?" She looks at me.

I nod my head.

I can feel my heartbeat picking up speed. My hands are trembling.

She's talking in Chinese. Everyone is quiet. It takes a while before she's speaking with someone who can help us. Now she's nodding her head and saying a lot of yeses. She's waiting. She motions for a pen and paper.

Marcy digs around in her bag and hands her the hotel notepad and a pencil. Amy writes something down. It looks like another address. She says thank you and hangs up. A smile is on her face.

"The orphanage moved to this address." She points to the one she wrote down. "I told them we wanted to visit. They don't usually allow visitors, but I explained your situation."

"Where is it?" Marcy asks.

"It's not far from your hotel. It's close to White Cloud Mountain."

I can't believe it. After all this driving, the new location was in the same area as our hotel. What are the chances?

Amy checks her watch, "We could be there by mid or late afternoon."

~

We run into some school traffic, and my eyes are getting heavy. I'm about to drift off, when Amy calls for the driver to slow down.

She glances at the address again and says, "We're here!"

I open my eyes and look at the new building in front of me. This one has three stories, clean windows, and fresh paint. There's a cute stone garden by the road.

We step out of the car and make our way up the stairs to the front door. Inside, Amy talks to someone who looks like they're in charge. As she's clarifying everything, I look around.

The building has a simple interior. There are some tables and chairs to the left of the front hall. Maybe that's where they eat meals. There's some artwork hanging on the walls. A few pieces look like they were made by kids; others look more professional. To the right, there's a longer couch and coffee table. Maybe that's a lounge area.

"Okay, she says we can go to the first and second floors." Amy is holding up a map of the house.

"What do you think's on the third floor?" Kate whispers.

"I don't know, but now I'm curious," I say.

I brace myself for whatever I'm about to see. We enter a common eating room. It's bigger than the space with tables and chairs that I saw earlier. Off to the side, there's a play area filled with baskets of toys and games.

We walk into a room that looks like it might be where school or tutoring happens. Maybe it's for the older kids. It just has four desks and maybe ten or so chairs. It doesn't look like a fully functioning classroom. There's only one small whiteboard on one of the walls.

We walk up a narrow staircase to the second floor. There, we see rooms for children of all ages. Most of the kids are girls, but there are a few boys here and there. Some are playing with each other. Others are sitting alone. My chest tightens and my vision blurs. That could have been me. I see nannies and volunteers with the youngest children.

An older nanny walks down the stairs from the third floor and looks at me. She tilts her head. I try to smile.

She makes her way to us and says to Amy in Chinese, "What's her name?"

I understand her, so I respond. "Leila. Or my Chinese name is Yìng Yuè."

She hears Yìng Yuè and her eyes light up. It's almost like she remembers me. She starts rapidly questioning Amy. I study her face. She looks familiar somehow, but how could that be? Could I remember her from when I was at the orphanage? But that's impossible, right?

Amy translates, "This is Líng Líng. She remembers a baby named Yìng Yuè. The little girl had sickly pale skin. She had your round face and a jagged birthmark on her right shoulder.

In Líng Líng's first year here, she was assigned to care for one girl who wasn't doing very well. She thinks it was you."

Is this true? Does Líng Líng really remember me? I have a jagged birthmark on my right shoulder. It's just barely visible under my white t-shirt. I look at Kate. Her mouth is open and her eyes wide. Marcy has her hand covering her mouth in amazement.

Líng Líng moves to stand right in front of me. We stare at each other. She wraps her arms around me and gives me a gentle squeeze. It's weird, but I feel like I remember this woman holding me. Maybe it's my brain playing tricks on me, but I don't mind.

"Do you know anything about my birth parents? Before I came here?" I look at Líng Líng. Amy is working hard to help us communicate.

"No, when she came here, you had already arrived. All she knows is that you were found in front of the old orphanage in a basket and wrapped in a blanket. There was no name, no letter, nothing."

That's almost exactly what my parents told me. I guess they were right.

"Do you know why nothing was left with me? Is there any way to find my birth parents?"

Líng Líng is shaking her head.

"Your parents were maybe afraid if anyone found out they left you. It was illegal to leave children even though the...one-child policy. If your parents had a first child, you could be... financial...ruin. The fine for a second child was more than many families could afford." She pauses. "Other punishments for not having an... abortion, might be losing jobs, homes, and belongings. It's a... miracle you survived, if you were a second child."

Amy is trying to help me understand in her broken, but clear English.

"Are there other reasons why they might have left me?"

"Traditionally... the boy carries on the family name. They

can make more money for the family and... take care of their parents in old age. Girls were married off and viewed as a... burden. Boys became more...valued than girls. If a girl was born ...a family might leave her... if they wanted a son."

She starts to fidget. "Other times...girls were left because of... disabilities. Families couldn't take care of them or... wanted to give them a chance for a better life. I don't know about you."

She looks uncomfortable as she talks about the reasons for abandoning girls. I'm still wondering why I was left.

"But there's no way to find them? Now that there's no longer the one-child policy?"

"It would be very difficult... Lots of time and money."

"Oh." I'm trying not to sound disappointed. I remember Huī Yīn. What about her? Is she here?

"Can you ask her if she remembers a girl named Huī Yīn? I think I was switched with her." Amy translates for Líng Líng.

Líng Líng grimaces. I take a deep breath, anticipating the worst.

Amy is trying to catch everything Líng Líng is saying. "She knew of a girl...Huī Yīn. She never talked to her, but heard rumors... from other nannies of a switch years ago. Líng Líng worked with the babies. Huī Yīn kept to... herself. Huī Yīn turned fifteen... she was released. It happened maybe...five months ago. Líng Líng was visiting her family when Huī Yīn left. She doesn't know what... happened to her."

Even though Líng Líng's not responsible for keeping track of Huī Yīn, I can't help feeling a little mad at her. How could she not know what happened to Huī Yīn? Where did Huī Yīn go?

"I...sorry," Líng Líng tries to say in English. She's looking down at the floor and her lip is quivering. I want to comfort her, but a part of me is still upset. How many girls have grown up in the orphanage and been forced to leave when they got too old? And now, no one cares to look for them or even keep track of them.

I'm on a rollercoaster of emotions. I was so close to finding

Huī Yīn, and just five months earlier I might have met her. It is what it is. Maybe it wasn't meant to be. We thank Líng Líng for her time, and she gives me another hug, but it doesn't feel as warm as before.

I gained some answers, but I'm left with more questions. I didn't find out anything about my birth parents. I still don't know why I was left, and I feel an even stronger mysterious connection to Huī Yīn.

Ling-Ling promises to check with the other nannies tomorrow to find information about Huī Yīn. I know now not to get my hopes up, but I can't help it. I feel like I'm so close.

It's a quiet walk back to the taxi. I think everyone can feel my disappointment.

As we're dropped off in front of the hotel, I give Amy one last hug. "Thank you for trying to help me get answers."

"I'm sorry that we couldn't find out what happened to Huī Yīn." We exchange contact information so we can stay in touch if she hears anything from Líng Líng.

~

On my phone, I see messages from Jasmine and my family asking how today went. I don't feel like responding. I'll find time to respond tomorrow at the airport.

"Do you want to go to dinner with the group?" Kate asks.

It's supposed to be a celebratory dinner together, but I don't feel in the mood to socialize.

"I'm just going to eat at the café."

"Are you sure?"

"Yeah, you should go though."

"Okay... let me know if you change your mind."

"Thanks for everything today."

"You would have done the same for me." She leaves the room key since I'll be back sooner, and heads out. After a brief visit to the café, I return to the room. I fall asleep watching a Chinese drama on TV. That night I don't dream of Huī Yīn. For the first time in a while, I can sleep through the night.

Part Three

Chapter 23

Yìng Yuè

I will miss China.

My time here was a whirlwind of excitement and let downs. Even though I didn't get all the answers I was looking for, I feel like I am beginning to understand myself more. I feel more connected to my culture and heritage. My only wish is that I had found Huī Yīn, but maybe there's still hope.

"How are you doing?" Kate asks.

"I'm okay. I think I'm ready to go home."

As we're waiting to board the plane, I respond to Jasmine and my family.

To Jasmine, *I found my orphanage. It was an experience getting there. Didn't find Huī Yīn, talk more when I'm back.*

To my family, *Found the orphanage, met one of the nannies, who remembered me. Her name is Líng Líng. Didn't get any answers about Huī Yīn. Still hopeful, maybe Líng Líng can find out.*

Goodbye Guangzhou. Until next time.

Connection

I woke up feeling
Strange
Like I wasn't
Myself
I was working with
Rose when I got
Dizzy
I
Stumbled
My vision got
Blurry
I sat
Down

I drank water
I waited
That feeling
Returned
Something was happening
Someone was
Here
But who?
I don't know
Anyone
What do they want?
It's gone
I feel nothing
I am alone

Líng Líng

Huī Yīn, someone is here to talk to you

Someone named Líng Líng.

Hello?

Huī Yīn. I'm Líng Líng. I work at your old orphanage.

I don't remember you.

I work on the third floor. We never met.

What do you want?

Someone was looking for you, yesterday.

Why? What's going on?

She thinks you were switched.

The other girl I remember, it was her! Where is she?

She left this morning to go back to America.

She's gone?

She wants to meet you.

How?

Here's her email. Do you have a computer?

I shake my head

Do you have a phone?

Yes

For work

She leaves a

Paper

I can send

HER

An email.

Other Girl

Why her?

Why does she want to

Talk?

What does she

Want?

Should I

Email?

Do I

Want to talk?

What if I say

No

What if I say

Yes?

Does she have

Answers?

Am I

Ready?

I will wait.

Maybe

Tomorrow.

Yìng Yuè (Leila)

"Welcome to Portland. The local time is 8:46 p.m., and the temperature is 42 degrees Fahrenheit. Thank you for flying with Air China," announces the captain.

The weather in China was so warm and pleasant. Now, back in Portland, I have to get used to the chilly temperatures again. I wonder how I managed the adjustment when I was first brought here.

Getting off the plane is a slow process. When we finally make it down the ramp, we go through customs as a group one last time, with Marcy leading the way. I see my parents waiting by the baggage carousel. I run to greet them.

On the drive home, Charlotte asks questions a mile a minute.

"So, what was it like? What did you do? Did you find Huī Yīn? Tell me everything."

And so, I retell my journey from start to finish. I describe the incredible food, the beautiful city, and the trek to my orphanage. I talk about the swim meet and the culture exchange with local students. I show pictures of the museums and temples and the White Swan Hotel. I give souvenirs from the White Cloud Mountain and Five Goats Statue.

Soon, we're back at our house. All the neighborhood Christmas lights are still up. They remind me of Guangzhou's night lights, although not nearly as magnificent.

~

Before I go to sleep, I look through my old baby pictures. There's me. Is Huī Yīn one of these other girls? Which one is she?

"Leila, is everything okay?" Charlotte looks at me.

"Yeah."

"You sure?"

"It will be."

"Okay... good night."

"Good night."

Rose's Push

Who was that
Yesterday?
Someone from the
Orphanage
What did she want?
Someone was looking for me
Another girl
She wanted to talk
We were switched
My story
Unfolds
I talk
And talk
I cry   Rose comforts
                She
                Hugs me
                Listens
                Waits
                I'm quiet
Will you do it?
Write to her?
I don't know.
I'm
Scared.
What do I say?
It'll come.
Maybe it will help

The Email

Should I do it?

I open my email

Is this safe?

I don't know her

Líng Líng does

She met her

Leila122803@gmail.com

What to say?

What to write?

Translator app

Chinese to English

Hello
My name is Huī Yīn.
You look
For me?
Líng Líng give me
Email.
What do you
Want?

Chapter 24

Yìng Yuè

The sun is streaming in through my blinds when I wake up. I didn't think I would sleep in after all the sleep I got on the plane, but I guess my body was tired from everything that has happened recently. I look over; Charlotte is already up and gone. Maybe she went to hang out with her friends. I hear my parents making breakfast downstairs. The coffee maker goes off and my stomach grumbles.

"Good morning!" My dad adds some cream to his coffee.

"How'd you sleep?" My mom is at the griddle flipping French toast.

"Okay."

"Do you want some?"

"Sure. Thanks."

She places two slices on a plate, and I grab a knife and fork from the kitchen drawer. I sit down and pour rich maple syrup over my pieces of French toast. It's warm and gooey. Mm, even though I was only gone a week—no, less than a week—I still missed this classic American breakfast.

I'm thinking about Huī Yīn, when my phone dings. It's Jasmine.

Hey, how are you? I heard from Kate that you didn't find Huī Yīn. Want to talk?

I'm okay. Just eating breakfast. Maybe later. I hit send.

"Leila, is everything okay?" my mom asks.

"We're sorry you weren't able to find Huī Yīn." My dad tries to comfort me. "But it was pretty unlikely. Maybe Líng Líng can track her down in a few days."

"Yeah. I know."

"Are you glad you went?"

"Yes."

"We're glad you got to go back. It's a beautiful city."

My parents leave to do some shopping and I go back upstairs to my room. I sit down at my computer and upload all my pictures from my trip. I click through them. So many memories in such a short time. I check my email. There's a new one.

Hello, my name is Huī Yīn… Wait, what? Is this really Huī Yīn?

I keep reading.

You look for me? Líng Líng gave me email. What do you want?

My jaw drops. I stare at the screen. I reread the email and then reread it again. Líng Líng found her! Huī Yīn wrote to me. What did I want? What would I say? I close my eyes and think. Then I start to type.

Dear Huī Yīn,

My name is Yìng Yuè…and Leila. I think I was adopted from the orphanage in your place. I think we were switched. I am so sorry. I wanted to find you. I wanted to meet you. I feel awful. Can you forgive me?

-Yìng Yuè

Response

An email

She replied

Her name is Yìng Yuè

She

Was adopted

Took my place

Took my home

She is sorry

Can I forgive her?

I feel

Angry

Hurt

She was a baby

It's not her fault

But

She had my

Life

It could have been

Me

I need

Time

Why?
Rose, why *her*?
Why not me?
It's my
Home
My
Family
Why?

Yìng Yuè

What do I do now? I found Huī Yīn, or, well, Líng Líng found her. Where was Huī Yīn? Was she still in the city? Was she angry with me? Could she forgive me? I text Kate and Jasmine.

Me: *I found her.*

Jasmine: *Wait, what?*

Kate: *You did? What are you going to do?*

Me: *I emailed her.*

Jasmine: *What did she say?*

Me: *She wanted to know why I was looking for her. I told her I think we were switched. It all happened so fast. I just sent the email. I don't know what to think.*

Jasmine: *Do your parents know?*

Me: *No, not yet. I'll tell them when they get back. I wish I could see Huī Yīn. I wonder what she looks like.*

Kate: *Do you think you could video chat with her?*

Me: *I don't know if she uses Facebook or FaceTime.*

Kate: *You could ask.*

Me: *True, maybe I'll ask her in the next email.*

Jasmine: *I can't believe you found her.*

Me: *Neither can I.*

Dear Yìng Yuè
I am upset.
But
It's not your
Fault.
Are you
Coming back?
Can I meet
You?

Dear Huī Yīn,

I understand. I am sorry this happened. I don't know when I'll be back. I would love to meet you too. Do you have FaceTime or Facebook?

-Yìng Yuè

I feel partly to blame for everything that has happened. I can't imagine what she is going through. I wonder what she is doing now. Did she stay in Guangzhou? Does she have a family? I hope we can video chat and talk face to face. Maybe I can go back to China sometime… Sometime soon.

Video Chat
What you mean?
FaceTime? Facebook?
No, I don't
Have them.
WeChat?
Video call?
Talk through that?

Dear Huī Yīn,

I know about WeChat. We can try video calling through that. When can you talk? What time works for you?

Time

Work 8-6

Dinner 6-7

Break 7-8

English 8-9

Time off?

Video chat at 7?

What time is it

There?

Is that okay?

Huī Yīn,

7 p.m. your time is 4 a.m. my time. It's kind of early, but if that's the only time you can do it, I can get up. Does tomorrow work?

Yes
Okay, try
Tomorrow 7 p.m.
See you
Tomorrow.

Chapter 25

Yìng Yuè

I wake up at 3:45 a.m. to get ready for the video call with Huī Yīn. I'm a ball of nervous and excited energy. What does she look like?

I take my laptop downstairs. It's eerily dark outside, and everyone is still sleeping. I plug in my headphones and log onto my laptop. I open WeChat. There's Huī Yīn, she's online. Here we go.

"Hello?" she answers the call.

"Huī Yīn? It's Yìng Yuè."

"Hi."

Through the screen, I see Huī Yīn. Her straight black hair is short, trimmed to a pixie cut. It frames her face. She has pale skin and a tiny nose; like mine. She smiles without her teeth showing. I sense confused emotions swirling around in her dark brown eyes. There's an instant connection, like an invisible thread linking us.

"How are you?" I ask.

"I am...well. How are you?" she says slowly.

"I'm good. I'm so happy I found you."

"Do you live... America?" she asks.

"I live in Portland, Oregon in the USA. Where do you live?" I try to slow down my talking so she can understand me better.

"I live at senior home. I work." Her English is getting more fragmented.

"Are you still in Guangzhou?"

"Yes. Guangzhou."

"Is your birthday July 18th, 2003?" Remembering the date on my passport, I want to see if it's her birthday.

"Yes... How...?"

"Your name and birthday were given to me when we were switched."

"Oh."

"Why did you leave the orphanage?"

"I too old. I had...go."

"Oh, I'm sorry."

Líng Líng was right. She had aged out and had to leave the orphanage. I feel so bad for Huī Yīn. I can't imagine the life she had. And now at fifteen she was already having to work a full-time job. What about school?

"Do you go to school?"

"No, I want." She sighs. "... No money."

"Oh, but your English is good!"

"Thank you, I...learn...at night."

"I wish there was something I could do to help you. You really want to go to school?"

"Yes, but I have work... here."

"Maybe I could send you money?"

"Maybe."

"I could help you with English too. I'll do anything I can to help you."

"Thank you."

"What do you like to do?"

"I like ...piano. Rose teach me."

"Who's Rose?"

"She lives here... I help her."

"Can you play something for me? I would love to hear you play."

"Not now."

"Oh, maybe later?"

"...Maybe."

The conversation starts to slow down. We're not sure what to say to each other.

"I go...soon."

"Can we do this again?"

"Ok."

"Thanks for talking to me."

"You...welcome. Bye."

"Bye."

We both sign off.

It was like reuniting with a long-lost sister. I had always dreamed that I had a sister out there. I used to pretend I was a twin and we would find each other somehow... After learning that I was switched, I felt this overwhelming sense of guilt about everything that happened. And I still do.

I wish there was more I could do to help her. It sounds like she really wants to go to school. Maybe sending money will work. I'll ask my parents when they get up.

Yìng Yuè
She seems nice
She wants to help
I can't stay mad
Maybe she can help
I want to go to school
I want to learn
There's so much more
Than working here

Music

I sit down

I don't know what I'm doing

My hands fly

I'm in a trance

I feel the music

"That's beautiful!"

Oh, Rose!

"You are improving!"

"What song is that?"

I shrug my shoulders

I don't know

She listens

I play

I am happy

Maybe my life will

Change

Yìng Yuè

While everyone is sleeping, I try to think of ways I could help Huī Yīn. I google the school we visited during the trip and find out the tuition is $15,000 USD a year! I don't have enough money to send Huī Yīn to school on my own. I never realized how fortunate I am to go to school for free.

While Huī Yīn could try enrolling in a cheaper public school, the quality of education isn't as good. After everything she's been through, I want her to have the best. But I don't have enough money, and I don't think my parents would be willing to send that much over to Huī Yīn. What else could I do?

Is adoption still out of the picture? What if my parents adopted Huī Yīn? I mean, it couldn't be that hard, right? They did it with me. I know they probably weren't thinking of having another kid, but Huī Yīn is different.

She doesn't have any family there. Here, she has me. She needs a home, and she wants to go to school. If she came here, she could have all of the opportunities I have. I send her a message through WeChat to see what she thinks of the idea.

What if my family adopted you? How would you feel about that? Do you want to come to the US and live with us? I know there's a lot we would have to work out... Let me know.

-Yìng Yuè

Adoption

I see a message
From Yìng Yuè
Adopt me?
Sigh
I shake my head
I am too old
I cannot be adopted
That's why I
Had to leave
It's too late
It's the law

Yìng Yuè

Even though I've been up since four, I don't feel tired. I think all the adrenaline is keeping me energized. There's so much to talk about. I can't hold it in any longer.

"So, I talked to Huī Yīn today," I start. "And I found out that she's living in a senior home. She has to work, but she wants to go to school, but she can't afford it, and she's learning piano from Rose and English... And I was thinking what if we adopted her?" I'm out of breath from talking so fast.

"Wait, hold on." My mom takes a sip of her herbal tea. "Adopt Huī Yīn?"

"That's a lot to ask when we don't even know her," my dad says thoughtfully.

"But it's not right that she's there all alone, and I'm here living her life. She would be here if we hadn't been switched."

"Leila, you have to stop blaming yourself for what happened. It's not your fault. We didn't know what was happening until it was too late. I know you feel guilty, but we can't just adopt her. There's so much legal work that would need to get done, and we don't know if she wants to be adopted," my mom points out.

"Well what can we do? Huī Yīn is my same age and working at a senior home. We can't just leave her there."

"I know. This is a lot for all of us, but you said yourself that Huī Yīn seems to be doing okay there. It's not the easiest life, but she's trying to learn English and piano from ...Rose? It might be best to just leave her where she is thriving," my dad says.

"But dad, she is NOT thriving. She shouldn't have to be working at a senior home. She wants to do so much more with her life, but she has never had the opportunity to try. I took that away from her."

"Okay, thriving was the wrong word. Leila, we know how hard this must be for you, but please, you need to calm down, and we need to research some options before we make any big decisions," my dad says with finality.

"You don't understand! How could you! You weren't the one who was switched. You are not responsible for another girl never being allowed to live her life."

I know I'm not acting my age, but I'm just so frustrated. I can't talk to them anymore. I need to do something. I run upstairs and slam my door. A few moments later, Charlotte pops her head in to see what was going on.

"Is everything okay?" she asks.

"No, Mom and Dad just don't get it. I feel like I need to do something for Huī Yīn after everything I took from her."

"Oh. But it's not like you stole her life. Not intentionally anyway."

"I know. But I thought I could make up for it if we adopted her and she came to live with us."

"Did you talk to her about it?"

"I sent her a message. I haven't heard back yet. Mom and Dad don't think it's a good idea."

"Maybe you should wait until you hear from her. What if you were her? What would you want?"

"I would want to come here."

"Think about Huī Yīn. All she's ever known is her life in China. How would you like it if you were suddenly taken from everything you knew? If you were flown to a new country where you didn't know the language?"

"But she's learning English, and it's really good already."

"Right, but we can't just take her out of China and bring her here. You can't expect that to make everything alright. She hardly knows you. You talked to her once?"

"Yeah... When did you become so wise?"

"Wow, the younger sister is counseling her elder."

"Hey, watch it," I grumble.

My phone dings. A new message; it's from Huī Yīn.

I'm too late. Adoption is no longer an option now. And maybe my plan wasn't that great, but deep down, I felt like if she were adopted and came to live here with us, everything would be okay. But it's not. We can't even adopt her if we wanted to. I don't know what to do.

"Hey, what is it?" Charlotte asks.

"We...can't adopt her." I'm trying to keep my emotions in check.

"Oh, I guess that answers that."

"How can you be so insensitive?"

"I'm not; I'm just being honest."

"Can you just leave?"

"I'm just trying to help."

"Charlotte, please. Before I say something I don't mean."

"Okay." She closes the door behind her.

I need some time to think, and I need to calm down. I slow down my breathing. In through my nose, out through my mouth. I guess I was getting my hopes up over an unlikely possibility. Charlotte and my parents are right. I don't know what I was thinking. I guess I just thought adoption would be the answer. It had worked for me, so why wouldn't it work for her? But I wasn't being realistic.

My parents knock on the door.

"Can we come in?"

"Yeah."

"Charlotte just told us we can't adopt Huī Yīn."

"Yeah."

"Leila, we know how much this means to you, but it sounds like it's a tricky situation. Nothing can happen in a day," my mom says.

"Right now, it's good that you and Huī Yīn have a way to stay in touch. It's not going to be easy, but we'll try to help Huī Yīn if we're able to," finishes my dad.

They hug me. "It's going to be okay. Huī Yīn will be okay."

Chapter 26

Huī Yīn

Hope
What is this feeling?
I haven't felt this
In *forever*
I am happy
To be alive
There are
Possibilities
I can do this
I have a
Friend
I am not alone

I Will Master English
I took the night off
I visited the
Language center
My English teacher was there
It's so good to see you!
Back again?
I nodded
Yes, I'm ready.
I will master
English
It's my chance
I will take it
It will help
Me
Get a better
Life

Rose

That night I was gone
I was learning
English
I never knew
Rose would collapse
She fell
Down the stairs
She couldn't
Call for help
Her heart
Gave out
They took her to the
Hospital
She is in a coma
Tears fall
Why?

Sadness

Rose died in her sleep
She will never again
Play piano
She will never again
Hear music
She will never again
Teach me
I have lost my teacher
I have lost a part of me
It's all my fault
I was gone
Do I deserve to learn?
Goodbye, Rose
I miss you

Mourning

I don't know if I can do this
I need strength
I need courage
I need hope
I don't know how much more I can take
When will I give up?
When will I say it's over?
When will enough be enough?

Two Weeks Later

Huī Yīn, you need to eat

Try to get some sleep

Take the day off

Get some rest

Play some music

Find something that makes you happy

Do you have anyone to talk to?

Where is your family?

My family?

Where are they?

Who are they?

Piano

I can't bear to touch the keys
I can't bear the sight of the piano
But I must
I need to move on
Rose would want me to
She believes —
Believed in me
I will play for her
In her memory
In her honor
I touch the keys
I start to play
I don't stop
I can't
I won't

Message from Yìng Yuè
How are you?
What have you been up to? I haven't heard from you
in a while.
Do you need anything?
Love,
Yìng Yuè

How to Respond

So many emotions

What to say?

Rose is dead

I am alone

You are so far

Will I ever make it?

When will my life change?

What can I do?

What is there to do?

I am grateful for you

But

What to say?

How am I?

I don't know

When will you be back?

Huī Yīn

Chapter 27

Yìng Yuè

I feel terrible. Rose was almost like family to Huī Yīn. Through Rose's music lessons Huī Yīn could escape her tiresome life, at least for a little while. Why is Huī Yīn's life so unfair? When will she catch a break?

Do I deserve to be happy right now? I wish I could do more. I need to make things right. I am living what could have been her life.

After hours of brainstorming and some heated discussions, my parents and I agree on starting a fundraising campaign for Huī Yīn. We're not sure of all the details yet, but tomorrow I'll be returning to school, and I'll try to balance the fundraiser with classes.

"Maybe you can talk to Mrs. Demore about turning your adoption project into a service project?" my mom suggests.

"Or you could talk to your new Communication teacher about sharing Huī Yīn's story with the community," my dad pitches.

The hope is that once people know about Huī Yīn, they'll be willing to help support her dream of a formal education. I still have Marcy's contact information from the trip. I'll see if she can help me get in touch with the school we visited. I'm hoping they might be willing to sponsor Huī Yīn after they hear her story. Huáměi would be the perfect school for Huī Yīn, if they will give her a chance.

I've decided to take a break from swimming for now. Even though my club practices will be resuming, helping Huī Yīn is more important.

My message to Huī Yīn goes like this.

Huī Yīn,

I have a new idea. I know, not all of my ideas are good. But hear this one out. What if I write about our switched story and share it with my community? I could create a GoFundMe page for you, and when people read about what happened, they might be willing to donate to your cause. I want to help you go to school and keep learning English. I don't want you to have to work anymore. It's just not fair. I will also try to contact the Huáměi International School that I visited in Guangzhou. I think you would like it there, but it's very expensive. I want to see if they can give you a scholarship. How does this sound? How are you doing? Sorry about the long message.

Love,
Yìng Yuè

News
Yes, that's a great idea
Anything will help
I can save up
For that school
I miss Rose
Thank you
For helping
Me
I am playing
Piano
More and more
It helps

Yìng Yuè

I email Marcy about the international school. She responds by the end of the day.

> *Leila,*
>
> *Yes, I would be happy to help. I have forwarded your email to the English program at Huáměi. Keep me posted. I'd love to help you in any way that I can.*
>
> *All the best,*
> *Marcy*

I'm excited. Things are in motion.

~

Jasmine: *Hey, can't wait to see you tomorrow!*
Kate: *You too!*
Me: *Meet at the courtyard. Lots to tell you.*

~

I'm sitting at the picnic table in the courtyard waiting for Kate and Jasmine. There's a thin layer of frost covering the ground, and I breathe out clouds of steam. I shiver; it's freezing out here. I miss the warm winter in Guangzhou.

"Hey, what's the news?" Kate steadies herself after almost slipping on the icy stone path.

I share everything that transpired yesterday.

"Wow, that's amazing. Let me know if there's anything I can do to help," Kate says.

"Yeah, me too. I could help set up the GoFundMe page. The cheer team has one for our State competition, so I know all about it," Jasmine adds.

"Thanks! That would be great."

The bell rings, and we carefully make our way to class across the icy campus.

At the end of third period, I approach Ms. Roth about my idea. For our first assignment in Communication, she wants us to research and write a feature article. She will select the top five to be submitted to the *Portland Times*. I couldn't have asked for a more perfect assignment.

"Ms. Roth, I know the rough draft of the feature article isn't due until next week, but I already have a story in mind. I'm trying to help a friend in China, and I want the story to reach as many people as possible. If I send you my article in a few days, do you think we could try to submit it to the Times sooner?"

"I don't see why not. We'll have to make sure it's newsworthy and meets their standards. Can I ask what you'll be writing about?"

"Well, I recently found out that when I was adopted, I was switched with another girl in the orphanage. I was adopted instead of her. Last week, when I was in China for the swim trip, I tried to track her down. I was able to video chat with her recently and learned about how hard her life has been since the switch. I want to try to help her go to school, because I know she wants to but never got the opportunity."

"Wow, it's incredible that you found her."

"She doesn't have any family, and I thought maybe if people knew about her story, they would be willing to donate to her cause."

"I can't promise they'll publish it, but I have a friend in the Lifestyle department who I think might be interested. Let's talk tomorrow and I'll let you know what I find out."

"Thank you so much!"

~

After school, I check in with Mrs. Demore. She agrees to let me use all the work I'm doing to help Huī Yīn in place of my final adoption project for her class. I go home feeling satisfied with everything that I accomplished today. Despite the cold weather, I'm feeling a little bit warmer inside. I am one step closer to helping Huī Yīn. I wonder if she is still playing music.

Solace

I must move on with my life
I can't mourn forever
I still think about her
Constantly
Music once helped me
Maybe it can help me again
I sit down on the piano bench
I think of Rose
This is for her
I start playing
It's nothing
I have learned
It is something brand new
My fingers move
I don't know what I'm doing
Have I just composed?
I write down the piece in my head
It goes like this…

Attachment

Dear Yìng Yuè,
I just wrote a song for Rose,
I know she will never hear it,
But I wanted to share it
With you,
Here it is…
-Huī Yīn

Chapter 28

Huī Yīn

News
Huī Yīn
The Director wants to see you
Why?
What did I do?
Huī Yīn
I have some news
Rose had a will
She comes from a wealthy family
She named you in her will
She left you her home on
Shāmiàn
Is this real?
I can't move
Huī Yīn, are you listening?
I nod.
Rose's nephew will be here soon
He wants to see you
Okay
You can take the day off
Thank you

Rose's Nephew

Are you Huī Yīn?

Yes

I am Rose's nephew

Zhāng Wěi

You are in her will

She left her home

To you

Why me?

She loved you

Like a daughter

She never had kids

Oh

I start to cry

Do you want to see her home?

I nod.

I can't talk

I need to sit down

Rose's Home
It's beautiful
On Shāmiàn Island
Grand but
It's home
Two floors
So many windows
A balcony?!
I miss Rose
I wish I could
Hug her
One last time
We go inside
There's not much
But she
Wanted you to have it
This is for you
Here is the key
How can I ever thank her?
Do you want to go upstairs?
I nod

A Piano

I walk upstairs

Paintings fill the hall

There are three rooms

One door is open

Inside is

A piano

It is so big and

Dusty

When was it last played?

I want to touch it

I am drawn to it

So elegant

It has history

I sit down on the bench

I touch the keys

They are soft

I start to play

Music fills the room

I don't want to stop

Rose's nephew watches

In awe

That was beautiful

Gratitude

Zhāng Wěi leaves

He will be back

Tomorrow

I wave goodbye

I am alone

I am

Home

Thank you

Rose

For everything

Chapter 29

Yìng Yuè

I listen to Huī Yīn's song. It transports me to another reality. I close my eyes, and we're together, traveling the world. Sisters, both doing what we love. She's playing piano at the most prestigious competitions, and I'm competing as a national swimmer. We're following our dreams, and we're happy. When her song finishes. I'm speechless.

I have another idea. What if we recorded Huī Yīn's music? I bet people would pay to hear her play. She has such a delicate touch, and her music is filled with emotion. It tells a story so much better than my words.

I send Huī Yīn a message about sharing her music with the world. We would have to figure out the money stuff to get it recorded, but potentially it could be another way to raise money for Huáměi.

Now, I need to get back to my article. Where do I start? How do I write my own story?

I start at the beginning...

Switched Sisters

Fifteen years ago, two baby girls were born. They each were born in different places but ended up at the same orphanage. For a brief time, they were together. One was sick and cried all the time, the other was quiet and lonely.

One was supposed to be adopted, but the other was put in her place.

That girl was me. I never knew I was switched, but when I was invited to swim in China, my life changed forever. I learned of my switched sister, of the girl who I never knew but was somehow connected to.

I looked for her in Guangzhou, but our efforts were futile. At the end of the trip I returned home to Portland. Somehow, by chance and perseverance, we found each other. I saw her through a screen. We talked and I learned of her story, her life at the orphanage.

At fifteen, she had to say goodbye to the only home she had ever known. She had to move to a senior home and work as a caretaker.

Now, Huī Yīn is an amazing young woman. Despite everything thrown at her, she remains strong. She is resilient. She is inspirational.

But she cannot do this alone. She needs help. If you are able to, after reading this article, I encourage you to donate what you can to help her go to school. She has never received a formal education, but she is so capable. She deserves one. You can donate on GoFundMe: School4HuīYin. Thank you.

Well, I had to leave a lot out, but here's to my first draft. I send it to Jasmine and Kate. They give me a thumbs up. Jasmine helps me set up the GoFundMe, and I add the song Huī Yīn recorded to the page. I look over my article one more time before sending it on to Ms. Roth.

~

"Leila, this is great! I edited a couple things, but I think it's a good start. I'll send this to my friend at the *Portland Times*. She'll probably edit it some more, and hopefully it can be printed in the Sunday issue. Thank you for sharing your story with us. You should be proud of all that you are trying to do for Huī Yīn."

"Thanks Ms. Roth. That means a lot."

~

Huī Yīn,

You won't believe it! I'm writing our story for the Portland Times! I hope to get it printed in the upcoming edition. I think this will work. People will want to help you. How are you? Have you thought about my idea some more? To sell your music? Your gift needs to be shared; it is amazing!

Love,
Yìng Yuè

Dear Yìng Yuè

You won't believe it
I think my luck is changing
Rose left me her home
It's on Shāmiàn Island
It is more than I
Have ever had
I am in her will
I quit my job
I won't work at the senior home
Anymore
Rose has a piano
It is beautiful
I am playing
I am writing for her
I want to keep playing
Thank you for everything
I want to share my music.

Composing

To Rose

I play and play
I don't stop
Zhāng Wěi arrives
He listens and
He watches
He records my song
On his phone
We listen
It is beautiful
It is her

You Could Do This

Your music is amazing
You could record it
And sell it
I know someone
Who could help you
What do you think?
Your talent is so incredible
Rose would be so proud
Thank you

Recording

In the morning
Zhāng Wěi takes me
To a recording studio
I play for his friend
She agrees with him
I could sell my music
She can't believe
I wrote my own songs
She listens
She is thoughtful.
She wants to
Record me
She will help me
Thank you
It pours out of me
My soul is
Released
Through music
I can't stop
It is my life
It is me
Huī Yīn

Recording Studio

I'm sorry
We can't take you on
As an artist right now
I love your music
Maybe in a few years
You can try again
I understand
Good luck.

Luck

What is luck?
One moment it is here
The next it is gone
Where does it go?
Why does it never stay?

YouTube
Zhāng Wěi
Films me
Playing piano
We send the videos to Yìng Yuè
She posts them on
YouTube
We wait
And wait
I wait
And wait

Yìng Yuè

"Good news! Your article will be printed in the Sunday paper," Ms. Roth tells me after class.

"Really? I can't believe it!" It's actually happening! Maybe I will make a difference in Huī Yīn's life.

"Thank you for everything Ms. Roth."

I open WeChat. Huī Yīn responded and sent me more clips of her playing her own music. I want to keep listening to the songs on repeat. Her music is indescribable. I feel everything she's feeling through her music.

I email Ms. Roth.

Can I add one more thing to the article?

Yes, if you send it immediately.

I add one more thing.

Huī Yīn is a gifted musician, and she is now writing her own music. I've included the YouTube link of her playing. If you want to support her music, please share this with everyone you know.

Maybe hearing Huī Yīn's talent will get people even more invested in her story and willing to donate.

Views
People are watching
I see the numbers growing
They like my music
They comment
They want more
I am not invisible
They like
My music

More

Do I have more in me?

What will I write?

What will I play?

I sit down.

It flows

Chapter 30

Yìng Yuè

I am watching Huī Yīn's YouTube channel grow. She sends more and more music each day. I think she has finally found her passion and her calling. From what I can tell, she seems much happier than when I first met her. She is no longer the timid girl I met a month ago.

My article in the Times blew up. People contacted the paper, wanting to help any way they could. They donated to her GoFundMe page, and they shared her YouTube videos.

Me: *We just hit $15,000!*

Kate: *Wow!!*

Jasmine: *That's enough for one year, right?*

Me: *Yeah, it's a good start.*

Jasmine: *My grandparents were in Salem and saw your story in the local paper.*

Me: *That's awesome!*

I guess my—no our—story is spreading fast. Maybe all of Oregon will be interested in helping.

My phone buzzes.

Dear Leila,

I am from the Oregonian Record Studios. I am interested in signing Huī Yīn on as an artist with my recording agency. How can we get in contact with her?

Thank you,
Jay

This seems too good to be true. Of course, I knew she was talented, but to have an agent want to contact her? This is amazing! I write immediately to Huī Yīn.

Your GoFundMe was a success! We reached our goal for the first year of school, and someone's interested in recording your music! He wants to sign you on as an artist. You could sell your music! I will put you in contact with him. His name is Jay, and he's from the Oregonian Record Studios. I am still waiting to hear back from Huáměi about a scholarship. I will let you know when I hear from them.

Yìng Yuè

Jay
I open WeChat.
One from Yìng Yuè
A record deal?
Someone wants to help me?
Sell my music?
His name is Jay
Can I do this?
Is my luck
Changing
Again?

The Deal

We message back and forth
Less than a week
Jay flies out to Guangzhou
He meets me
He listens to my songs
He talks about a contract
Zhāng Wěi helps translate
Jay thinks I have talent
He thinks I could
Sell albums
Lots of them
He wants me to start
Now   I would have to come to
America
To record
My music
I can't leave
I don't have a passport
Where would I stay?
I have never left
Guangzhou
He promises to
Help
His company will help
Organize the papers
Do I agree?
I have two days

Two Days

I talk to Zhāng Wěi

He thinks it's a good contract

He thinks it will be good

For me

I talk to Yìng Yuè

She loves the idea

She wants me to

Stay with her when

I go to America

She will help me

Get around

I can't believe this

Am I dreaming?

What if something happens?

If it all disappears?

It doesn't work?

I fail?

I can't sell

Music

If I move

Can I come back?

Will I return to Guangzhou?

What about school?

Can I still go?

I want to play music

I want to go to school

Can I do both?

Do I have to choose?

I need to talk to

Jay

The Choice

If I go to America
Can I come back to
Guangzhou?
Yes, of course!
You only need to be
In Portland while you record
Then you can come back
I don't have money to fly
It's in your contract
We would pay for you to fly
Back and forth once a year
For five years
Five years?
Yes, you will need to record music
Once a year for five years
That's a long time
Can I do this for five years?
I think I can
Can I still go to school?
Yes, you can
In Guangzhou?
Yes.
Okay
This sounds good
I can do both.
I will do both.

Signature
You read the contract?
I nod my head
You agree?
Yes
Sign here.
Deep breath.
Okay
Here I go
I sign
In Chinese and
English
It's done
I did it

Guangzhou to Portland

I get my picture taken
I fill out paperwork
I wait and
Wait
Jay and Zhāng Wěi
Help
I have a passport
I have a visa
I have a
Ticket
Zhāng Wěi drives
Me to the airport
Thank you for everything
We hug
Goodbye
It's my first time on a plane

I'm nervous
The plane is shaking
We're moving fast
We're lifting
I hold my seat
Hold my breath
I close my eyes
It's okay
It's okay
I can do this
It's a long ride
Day to night to
Day
"Welcome to Portland."
I did it.
I made it
I am here in
The United States of America

Complete
Yìng Yuè's there
I see her
I recognize her face
Immediately
She's waiting for me
She waves
I have long
Forgiven her
It was not her
Fault
She's done so
Much for
Me
She's like the
Sister I never
Had
She's like
My other half

Yìng Yuè

Here we are, face to face, in person. Huī Yīn looks strangely calm, at peace. She slowly makes her way toward me. As she walks over, I notice her feet are turned inward and cause her to slightly limp. When she reaches me, we embrace. In an instant, it feels like a part of me has been restored. For so long I felt like something was missing. I wasn't complete. Until now.

Chapter 31

Huī Yīn

Another Family?
We go to her house
I meet her family
Everyone is so kind
They are friendly
They are welcoming
They are family

First Song

I go to the studio

I play

I listen

They talk

They want me to change it

I rewrite it

I play again

We listen

It's better

We continue

This continues

On and on

It's a long day

Am I done?

No

Come back tomorrow

This continues for

Two weeks

Night Out

Leila, Jasmine, and Kate
Those are her friends
Show me
Portland
We ride pink trolleys
We go downtown to the
Food carts
So many kinds of
Food
I have never tried
Quesadillas
Tamales
Lamb curry
Falafels
Lasagna
It all smells so different
So good

Day Adventures

We take a boat
Down the Willamette River
There's a giant bookstore
Powell's
Four floors of books
And more books
I have never seen so many
Books
I try American pancakes at the
Original Pancake House
They are fluffy and warm with
Soft butter and
Hot maple syrup
So sweet
Too sweet
Unlike anything I have had before
We visit Sellwood Docks and
Walk along the water
It's calm and
Peaceful
It's beautiful

First Album

I'm working a lot
When I'm not with Leila
I go to the studio
I play more music
Jay records more songs
I can't believe it's
Unlimited
It's endless
Hours and hours
Composing and composing
Changing and rewriting
Recording and playing
Critiques and opinions
You're done!
Congratulations
Finally
I'm done
It will be released
On my birthday
July 18th
Five more months
I can't wait

Swim Lessons

Do you know how to swim?
I shake my head
No, I never learned
My feet are bad
People used to laugh
Say I walked funny
I didn't think I could
I'll show you
Your feet are fine!
Yìng Yuè teaches me
I learn to float
On my stomach and
Back   I am weightless
It scares me   It's like magic
                              I hold my breath
                              I blow bubbles
                        Water goes up my nose
                              I try to kick
                              It's working
                              My feet are fine
                    Now move your arms like this
                              I try
                              I can do it
                              She helps me
                              It's not pretty
                              I am swimming

Goodbye
Thank you for
Letting me stay with you
Showing me Portland
Teaching me how to swim
Sharing your
Friends and
Family
I will miss you
But I will be back
In one year
For more recording
Thank you

Chapter 32

Yìng Yuè

I can't believe it has already been six months since I found Huī Yīn. After she got her record deal, she became a little celebrity around here. I've been staying in touch with her through WeChat. Two days ago, she sent a video that showed her composing more music.

I can't wait for the album to come out on her (maybe) birthday. I have goosebumps just thinking about it. She is getting the opportunities she deserves.

I have an appearance on the Portland Nightly News in less than a week, my first interview in a series to share the story of how I found Huī Yīn. Melinda, the host, wants me to send her an email about everything that has happened so she knows what to talk about during the interview.

Dear Melinda,

Back in March, Huī Yīn came to visit so she could record her first album. She stayed with my family, and I showed her around Portland. She came during spring break, so we got to hang out and explore. She met my friends, Jasmine, and Kate, and my sister Charlotte.

At our house, Huī Yīn practiced and composed on Charlotte's piano before going to the studio. She truly is a prodigy (at least I think so). I can't wait for the world to hear her. Music is her outlet, like how swimming is mine.

Through songs, she shares her voice and her — our — story. In her music, I feel as though I am living her life alongside her; from the switch, to growing up in the orphanage, to eventually reconnecting. Her visit was short, but she will be back. It's in her contract.

Oh, and I almost forgot to mention, Huī Yīn got a scholarship to Huáměi. It only covers tuition, but her record deal and the money from the GoFundMe should help to cover room and board. She's been able to work out a schedule with Huáměi and Jay so she can keep making music while going to school. This all almost feels like a dream, but I'm not complaining.

I look forward to being on your show,
Leila (Yìng Yuè)

~

I'm waiting for my turn to go on stage. The familiar clammy palms are back, and I'm focusing on my breath. I'm not feeling great, but I'm not doing this for me. I'm doing this for Huī Yīn.

After we get through introductions, I gradually feel more comfortable in the spotlight. Melinda's interviewing style is gentle, and I am starting to open up more. The world needs to hear our story: the truth about Huī Yīn.

~

The summer heat has arrived. In class, we have to open all the windows because it gets hot and smelly in our stuffy room with thirty growing teenagers. I should be focusing on Mr. Myers' geometry final, but all the formulas seem so insignificant compared to my summer plans.

I'm practically counting down the seconds until the last bell rings. When it does, I turn in my completed math final and happily walk out the door.

Kate and Jasmine are waiting by the courtyard, and we take the city bus to Salt and Straw, our new favorite ice cream shop.

"When's the flight?" Jasmine asks after she orders two scoops of honey lavender.

"Tonight at 8:45." I order one scoop of sea salt and caramel and one scoop of strawberry coconut.

"I wish I could go back," Kate says wistfully. She takes a bite of her cookies and cream.

"Maybe next time you both can come." I pick up a spoon and napkin. "Huī Yīn's going to be so surprised."

Summer School

Today is my first day of school
I am taking summer classes
To catch up on all the
Time I missed
I am going to
Huáměi International High School
This is my dream
I can do this
I will do this
My fingers tingle
I smile
I am alive

Yìng Yuè

After ice cream with Jasmine and Kate, I finish packing my suitcase. We pile into the car with all our bags. Charlotte is bringing her own checked suitcase and a carry-on even though we're only staying in Guangzhou for a month.

A wave of déjà vu hits me. How many times is this going to keep happening?

"This is so exciting!" Charlotte says as she hands the flight attendant her boarding pass.

"I know!" I can't contain the smile that spreads across my face. I settle in for the long flight ahead of us. What should I watch this time?

~

When we eventually land and make it through customs, no thanks to Charlotte and her endless complaints, Amy and Líng Líng are waiting for us by the airport exit. I run with my little red suitcase trailing behind me.

Amy and Líng Líng have become part of my family throughout all of this. There's a quick round of introductions, then Líng Líng drives us to Rose's, now Huī Yīn's, home.

I spot it from down the road. It's a magnificent townhouse. I don't know what Huī Yīn was talking about. It's not modest at all. I remember this row of colonial houses from my walk through Shāmiàn six months ago? I never would have thought my switched sister would be living here.

We wait at Huī Yīn's house while she finishes up with school for the day. As we are waiting, I can't stop pacing. In spite of all our video chatting, I am still anxious to see her again.

She opens the door and steps inside. Charlotte shouts, "Surprise!" I smile. My parents are the first to greet her. Huī Yīn has a healthy glow about her.

Hello

I hear people talking

The voices sound familiar

They're laughing

Is this what

Family

Is?

I open the door.

Resolution

We are together

Again

There's that connection

I feel it

We were separated

We are no longer

Apart

My switched

Sister

She is me

I am

Her

Birthday
It is July 18th
Today is my birthday (*I think*)
I am 16
Yìng Yuè is still here
I am content
Today my album is released
I am a musician
I am a student

Yìng Yuè

Dear Jasmine and Kate,

You know, we only planned on staying here for a month, but my parents said it would be a shame to go home so soon. There's still so much to do, and they don't want to leave Huī Yīn yet. So...we've decided to stay the rest of the summer!

Huī Yīn is trying to teach me piano again. Charlotte laughs at my attempts. I think I'm figuring out the basics. Huī Yīn is a good teacher, but I don't have the natural gift she has.

I have made peace with what happened to us and no longer feel as guilty as I once did about our switch. I still can't help feeling uncomfortable about it, even though I know that I had no control over what happened.

I am grateful that Huī Yīn doesn't hold a grudge against me. We have come so far. We found each other and healed together. I like to think I was able to help her reclaim her life and she helped me conquer mine.

Love,
Leila

P.S. Do you like this postcard? Kate, you'll recognize it. Jasmine, it's the sparkling Canton Tower at night.

New Life
My life has a new purpose
I have a second chance
To make my life
My own

Switched
I am not
Angry or
Sad
Hurt or
Bitter
I am
Strong and
Resilient
Happy and
At peace
I found
Love
I found
My Family

Epilogue

Yìng Yuè

At the end of the humid, tropical summer, I step onto the plane and wave goodbye to my first home. While I have not been able to learn anything about my birth parents, I found something better. I found my switched sister.

I enjoyed our time together, and I'm already looking forward to Huī Yīn's next visit. She promises to keep up with our weekly video calls between now and then, but I know our schedules will keep us both very busy.

I've decided to start journaling about my life. Who knows, maybe I'll turn it into a book one day.

September 22nd

The cool shift in weather marks the beginning of fall. Jasmine, Kate, and I are helping our team remain undefeated this season. Our relay this year is the three of us plus Sirena. Lacey and Oliva went off to college, but they drop by occasionally to say hi.

Jasmine couldn't stay away from swimming. She realized she still loves it as long as she swims on her own terms. Her mom is just happy she's back on the team. Jasmine continues to cheer and loves robotics. She even manages to find time to hang out with Kyle.

Kate is training to be a State champion in all of her events. She is constantly pushing me to keep up with her. She says she loves Portland and wants her relatives to visit soon. I hope they will.

Huī Yīn is still playing and writing music every day in Guangzhou. It's hard being away from her, but I hope to go back to visit during winter break.

Life in Portland is not the same as it was a year ago. I feel like I am not the same person I was then. I am no longer angry at the orphanage, because I realize that our experiences have turned us into stronger, braver young women. I have learned so much from Huī Yīn and she from me.

Huī Yīn inspires me to live my life, embrace the present, and appreciate all that I have. We still have our whole lives ahead of us. I don't know where we'll end up, but whatever happens we have each other.

Future
I am
Forever grateful to
Yìng Yuè
If she hadn't searched for
Me
I would not
Be who I am
Today
My life awaits
Thanks to
Her

And that is the story of two switched girls. We found each other against all odds, and our lives have been changed for the better.

The End

Acknowledgments

Thank you to all of the people in my life who have helped shape me into the strong, young woman I am. I would not have been able to write this book without you.

Thank you, Mom and Dad, for always being my personal editors on call and helping me get through some of the more emotional parts of this story.

Jenna and Karina: thank you for being my cheerleaders and supporters in Taiwan as I attempted to write this on those weekend café outings. Thanks for helping me with all things Chinese.

Anna and Saige: thanks for encouraging me to write my story and for helping me set it in Portland. You were there when this all began.

Leah: the cover art is incredible and thanks for carrying on the legacy of the WWU Adoptees.

Ming: thank you for our conversation about the one-child policy and for introducing me to the Seattle adoptees.

My GoFundMe donors, Bailey, Jane, Yi, Sada, Shannon, Scott, Hannah, Elisabeth, Kristen, Nicole, Marlene: you made this book a reality.

Dr. V: thank you for showing how much you care for your students, employees, and mentees.

Amy Sonnichsen: *Switched* would not have been written if not for *Red Butterfly*.

To my editors, publishers, and designers: it does take a team to share a story.

Thank **you** for reading *Switched*.

About the Author

Iris Báijīng Hubbard is a Chinese American adoptee from Guangzhou, China. She was given the name Báijīng in the orphanage, which means white crystal. Iris was adopted when she was about sixteen months old and grew up in Mount Vernon, WA.

Iris became more interested in learning about her adoptee identity while in college. There, she started a club for adoptees called the WWU Adoptees. Iris was indeed a competitive swimmer and today, she loves to bake and paint. This story is inspired by events from her life—close friends and family might be able to pick out the Easter eggs and fun facts scattered throughout this novel.

Iris is currently a master's student at the University of Eastern Finland studying early language education for intercultural communication.

CPSIA information can be obtained
at www.ICGtesting.com
Printed in the USA
LVHW042130301221
707552LV00010B/969

9 780578 767024